JEWEL BOX

Short Works by Mary Anna Evans

D1227930

Joyeuse Press

WILLARD LIBRARY, BATTLE CREEK, MI

Copyright © 2011 by Mary Anna Evans

Print edition – 978-1475226591
Other ebook editions – 978-0-9827092-5-2
Kindle edition – 978-0-9850401-1-6

All rights reserved. Without limiting the rights under copyright reserved above, no part of this publication may be reproduced, stored in or introduced into a retrieval system, or transmitted, in any form, or by any means (electronic, mechanical, photocopying, recording, or otherwise) without the prior written permission of both the copyright owner and the above publisher of this book.

This is a work of fiction. Names, characters, places, brands, media, and incidents are either the product of the author's imagination or are used fictitiously. The author acknowledges the trademarked status and trademark owners of various products referenced in this work of fiction, which have been used without permission. The publication/use of these trademarks is not authorized, associated with, or sponsored by the trademark owners.

"Low Budget Monster Flick" first appeared in *Florida Heat Wave*, edited by Michael Lister for Tyrus Books in Madison, Wisconsin.
©2010

"Land of the Flowers" first appeared in *A Merry Band of Murderers*, edited by Don Bruns and Claudia Bishop for Poisoned Pen Press in Scottsdale, Arizona.
©2006

"Twin Set"
©2005

"Yes, It Can Be Done: *The Caves of Steel* by Isaac Asimov" first appeared in *Mystery Muses: 100 Classics That Inspire Today's Mystery Writers*, edited by Jim Huang and Austin Lugar for The Crum Creek Press in Carmel Indiana.
©2006

"Stealing Mona" first appeared in *Mystery Readers Journal*, edited by Janet Rudolph.
©2004

"A Singularly Unsuitable Word" first appeared in *A Kudzu Christmas*, edited by Jim Gilbert and Gail Waller for River City Publishing in Montgomery, Alabama, and in *Offerings: 3 Stories by Mary Anna Evans* for Joyeuse Press in Gainesville, Florida.
©2005

"Mouse House" appeared in *North Florida Noir*, edited by Michael Lister for Pottersville Press in Panama City, Florida, and in *Offerings: 3 Stories by Mary Anna Evans* for Joyeuse Press in Gainesville, Florida.
©2006

"Starch" appeared in *Plots with Guns*, edited by Anthony Neil Smith, and in *Offerings: 3 Stories by Mary Anna Evans* for Joyeuse Press in Gainesville, Florida.
©2004

"The Final Radical" by Libby Hellmann first appeared in *Futures*. It has also appeared in Hellmann's collection, *Nice Girl Does Noir* (2010). ©2000

"Cally's Story" appeared in *Artifacts*, Poisoned Pen Press, Scottsdale, AZ
©2003

Wounded Earth, Joyeuse Press, Gainesville, FL
©1995

Cover design by Rickhardt Capidamonte

Author photo by Randy Batista

Back cover photo by Joe Flintham
Image: http://www.flickr.com/photos/joeflintham/4790411155

Print layout by eBooks by Barb for booknook.biz

Other works by Mary Anna Evans:

Novels, all available as ebooks and in print:

Wounded Earth, an environmental thriller

The Faye Longchamp archaeological mysteries:

Artifacts
Relics
Effigies
Findings
Floodgates
Strangers
Plunder

Collections:

Jewel Box, a book-length collection of short stories and essays, available in e-book and print editions

Offerings, an e-book mini-collection of short stories

Individual short stories, all available as e-books:

"Low-Budget Monster Flick"
"Twin Set"
"Land of the Flowers"
"A Singularly Unsuitable Word"
"Starch"
"Mouse House"

Educational non-fiction

Mathematical Literacy in the Middle and High School Grades: A Modern Approach to Sparking Student Interest

For Isaac Asimov and Alfred Hitchcock,
the gentlemen who introduced me
to the clear and focused art of
the short story

Acknowledgments

I'd like to thank Amanda Evans and Michael Garmon for reading this volume in manuscript. There are fewer errors than there might have been without their help. Those that remain are all mine.

I'm also grateful to Libby Hellmann for sharing her story "The Last Radical" with me and with my readers.

I'd also like to express my gratitude to the editors who first published the work in this volume: Barbara Peters, Ellen Larson, Anthony Neil Smith, Michael Lister, Janet Rudolph, Jim Gilbert, Gail Waller, Claudia Bishop (also known as Mary Stanton), Don Bruns, Jim Huang, and Austin Lugar. I'm grateful for their votes of confidence in publishing my work and for their help in making it the best work I could do.

TABLE OF CONTENTS

FOREWORD–WHY WRITE SHORT?

by Mary Anna Evans

I'm a novelist. I think I was born to be a novelist. Name a topic, and I have a whole lot to say on the matter. Ask me to express those opinions in a few pithy sentences, and I'm going to struggle.

Oh, I can do it. My agent tells me that I'm especially good at boiling the plot of one of my novels down to a synopsis consisting of a couple of tight and to-the-point pages. But I prefer to let my storytelling muse flow free... most of the time.

Between books, I like to write short stories. Stories and novels are completely different art forms, and I find that practicing one of those art forms hones my skills in the other. And I use the word "hone" intentionally.

To me, short stories are like jewels, finely honed and polished mirror-bright. This is why I chose *Jewel Box* as the title of this collection. When working with a few thousand words, as opposed to one of my 95,000-word novels, I can make sure that every single one of those words is intentionally chosen and set carefully in its place. Taking this notion to its extreme, I sometimes suggest to beginning writers that they take occasional breaks from their novels to write poetry. Confining one's thoughts to the fourteen lines of a sonnet or to the meager seventeen syllables of a haiku forces careful and exacting choices. A novelist needs those skills. Just because I have 95,000 words to work with, it doesn't mean I have license to be sloppy.

This is a collection of mystery short stories, and the mystery genre offers its own challenges. A story that offers a slice of life can be of any length, from a one-page short-short that describes a person's single moment of illumination to a multi-thousand-page depiction of the most important day in that person's life. But a mystery story...it has to offer the reader a question and a plot. It has to deliver enough clues to answer that question. As a writer, I sometimes despair over the difficulty of showing a crime and introducing suspects and dropping clues and resolving the mystery, all in just a few pages. But I do so love the challenge.

Join me and my guest, Libby Hellmann, in this jewel box of mystery stories. They were cut and polished just for you.

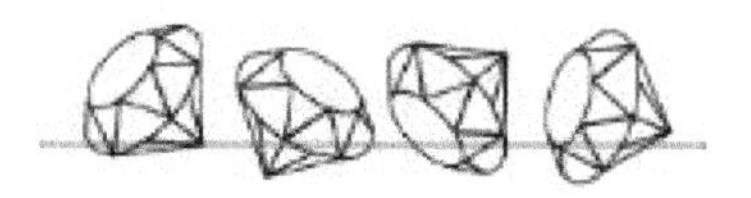

LAND OF THE FLOWERS

Florida is my adopted home, and this story is a love letter to that home.

In some ways, Florida isn't so different from my birthplace, Mississippi. In both places, summer is an interminable death march through air so hot and steamy that it's actually visible to the naked eye. As a result, I don't completely trust air that I can't see. To be truly secure, I need to feel it give me a wet and loving slap on the face when I venture out of my air-conditioned home.

Still, Florida has a touch of the exotic that south Mississippi does not. There are palm trees standing tall in the forests here, mixed in among the live oaks and longleaf pines. Gauzy Spanish moss drips from anything that stands still long enough to give the stuff a foothold. The conquistadors stepped ashore here and left behind cities with old Spanish names. And then there are the alligators....

– Mary Anna

LAND OF THE FLOWERS

A composting toilet.

Garrett Levy already knew more than he wanted to know about composting toilets. Environmental engineering had sounded like a glamorous career when he signed up for it, but the reality had been...well, he should have known that cleaning up a planet wouldn't be a walk in the park. Garrett had spent his years in graduate school learning how to treat various forms of toxic sludge, which meant that he'd spent an entire semester researching the intimate workings of composting toilets.

But he'd never seen one in a private home. Especially not a private home like this one. Congressman Joseph Swain lived in a rustic palace. A sprawling pile of wood and glass, it sat on pilings high above a riverine wetland. With broad eaves overhanging a vast outdoor living space, it was more porch than house. If there was a better place to host a hundred people for the weekend, Garrett couldn't imagine it.

Congressman Swain's voice echoed down the hall. "We wouldn't think of installing a septic system out here, even if we could get a permit. This delicate ecosystem could never process the volume of human waste we're generating here today. And people do seem to like my parties."

The congressman arrived on the heels of his rumbling baritone. He appeared to spend most of those parties taking guests on tours of his environmentally perfect home. Garrett had trailed along after him long enough to hear the first part of his spiel, then drifted away to check out the plumbing. It seemed that his proud tour guide had caught up with him. The bathroom was spacious, but it wasn't built for five. Garrett sidled toward the door, only to have his escape aborted.

"Welcome, Mr. Levy," the politician said, clapping a hand on his shoulder. "It's so good to have a representative of the Florida Department of Environmental Protection among us."

Garrett was impressed that the man knew who he was. He didn't ordinarily party with the movers-and-shakers, but his friend Ken had invited Garrett to meet him out here. Maybe Ken had told Swain earlier in the week that he was bringing a guest. Garrett's cell phone company had been a tad too slow in forwarding the message that Ken was home sick with the flu, so he was here alone, trying not to look like a short, balding wallflower.

"With your experience and training, Mr. Levy," Swain continued, "you can appreciate the things we do here. Solar panels give us electricity, water from the sinks is treated and sent to our spray field, and all our biodegradable waste is composted—food, paper, even...well, maybe we don't want to go into the details of this composting toilet."

A well-coifed redhead tittered.

"Composting toilets violate one of our most deep-rooted taboos—keeping our waste out of sight—but they make the best kind of sense. Why waste drinkable water for flushing? Not to mention the problems involved in disposing of treated waste from our sewage plants. Why not turn it into clean, sanitary compost, right in your own home, then use it to make the world around you greener?"

The redhead recoiled, then followed Garrett as he made his escape. "No wonder Wynnda hates this place," she muttered under her breath. Realizing she had an audience, she turned her bleach-enhanced smile on Garrett.

"Do you know that Wynnda says Joseph wants to be out here every single day the legislature's not in session? She told him to make himself at home, but she'd be staying in Tallahassee, where she has air conditioning and the bugs stay outside where they belong. And where she has a toilet that flushes." She shuddered and hurried downstairs to the bar.

Garrett strolled out on the balcony. He looked down at the throng gathered on the deck below. They milled around, like the insects that had converged on the congressman's open-air buffet. Hell, everything was open-air here.

In the far corner of the deck stood a cluster of women who, like the congressman's other guests, didn't belong in the swamp. This was not a place for lipstick or toenail polish, but five women with colorful lips and toes stood heads-together, whispering as if they thought they might be heard above the din of the crowd and the soaring melodies of the bluegrass band standing twenty feet away. He recognized Wynnda Swain at the center of the group. Her straight ash-blonde hair framed flawless, pale skin. She was exquisite and so, to Garrett's eyes, was this house and the wild land around it, but it was no setting for a woman like this one.

Congressman Swain led his tour group out onto the deck and gestured magnanimously toward the bar. He stood nearly a head taller than anyone else around him, and the sunlight caught his shock of white hair. Being handsome was a valuable political tool.

Another bunch of sycophants clad in chinos and deck shoes gathered around him. They were dressed appropriately for the boats that had brought them here, and those rubber-soled low-top shoes had carried them easily down the boardwalk leading from the river to the house, but they'd be wise to stay clear of the wetlands ringing the tiny, sandy spot of high ground that Swain had tamed. North Florida mud would suck the shoes right off their feet. Garrett didn't think he'd seen anyone at the party, other than him, wearing solid, sensible boots.

He looked down on Swain as he beckoned to Wynnda. Wives could also be valuable political tools, and the congressman had somehow coerced his to attend this party, but he was powerless to make her look happy about it.

An olive-skinned man, short and stout with powerful shoulders, staggered out the balcony door and leaned against the railing, standing about six inches closer than Garrett would have preferred. His personal policy was to keep drunks at least a couple of feet away.

Garrett noticed that, below his khaki shorts, the man's right lower leg was encased in a white plaster cast and a sandal-like apparatus was strapped around his foot, presumably to protect the cast from whatever its wearer might step in. The other foot was clad in a boot even more worn than Garrett's own. He rethought his snap judgment. Maybe the man wasn't drunk. He might be staggering under the influence of his lopsided shoes.

"God's got some sense of humor." The smell of beer hung around the man's head like an odorous halo. Garrett re-revised his opinion. His companion was quite inebriated.

Garrett, who'd learned not to encourage drunks who want to talk, allowed himself two words. "How so?"

"How else do you explain a hypocritical jerk like that one," he said, gesturing toward Swain, "being blessed with all this?" A stubby hand waved through the air, encompassing the spectacular house and its overhanging live oaks. Maybe the beautiful wife, too.

Garrett studied the palm-adorned uplands and the marsh and swamp that surrounded them, sheltering a river that was just out of sight. Nestled into the trees below the balcony where they stood was the crown jewel of Swain's property. In Garrett's considered opinion, no one man deserved to possess a piece of nature so beautiful, though he would give the congressman credit for sharing it with his partygoing friends.

From their perch on the balcony, Garrett and his drunken companion could gaze down into the opalescent depths of that jewel, a first-magnitude limestone spring. Glass-clear water poured out of the bowels of the earth into its basin, then overspilled into a channel that carried it through an open marsh, then into swampy woods and, eventually, into the river. Some of Swain's guests had donned scuba gear to explore the cavern that disgorged all that crystalline water. They were dozens of feet below the surface, but Garrett could read the logos printed across the backs of their swim trunks.

Named McGilray's Hole by a long-gone pioneer, Joseph Swain had possessed the great good sense to buy the property that sheltered it, back when he was a very young man and treasures like this one were still undervalued.

The story of how he built his own personal paradise here was well-known to anybody who read Florida newspapers. Swain had immediately begun the house, doing as much of the work himself as he could. He had cut the trees himself, taking out as few as possible and having them cut into the lumber that framed the structure that had become, for him, the ultimate recycling project. He'd taught himself to do construction work out of books. Then, when his legal practice took off, he had hired professionals to expand the original structure into the home of his dreams.

And he did it all before the wetlands protection laws went into effect that would have made building on this land impossible.

A thought struck him. Garrett squinted at the man at his side. "Did you say 'hypocrite'?"

"I did."

"Why?"

"I own the adjacent property, just upriver. Inherited it from my old man about ten years ago. I'd love to have a place like this."

"But you can't get a permit to build one?"

"Damn straight. As soon as Swain got his place just the way he wanted it, he spearheaded tough conservation laws through the legislature. No way he could build a house like this any more. Nobody else can, either. Look around. You see anybody else living out here? I can use my land for hunting and fishing, but that's about it."

Garrett looked across the pristine waters of McGilray's Hole, deep into the trees beyond. The swampy woodland floor was alive with a yellow blanket of late-summer sneezeweed. Here and there, the foamy white flowers of water hemlock rose up on stalks as tall as a woman. Was it any wonder the Spanish called this place *La Florida*—the Land of the Flowers? He couldn't say that he was sorry that his new friend wouldn't be able to tear up another chunk of Florida to build his house, but he could understand the man's position.

"How do the landowners in these parts feel about Swain's approach to environmental protection?"

"Every year, we pay our taxes on land we can't use. How do you think we feel?"

"They why are you at this man's party, Mr.—"

"Marquez. Stan Marquez."

"I'm Garrett Levy."

The man stuck out a hand dripping with water that had condensed on the surface of his mug. "Why am I here? For the free beer?" He chuckled. "I called all the land-owners up and down the river when I heard Swain was having another one of his open-house shindigs. I told them that the congressman needed to see us, face-to-face. There would've been no need to say anything to him—he knows who we are. I just wanted him to remember that we live here too, and that we vote. Nobody but me had the guts to show up."

"Do you think it would have helped if your friends had come?"

Marquez snorted. "Hell, no. He doesn't need us and we all know it. Swain built his career on the environmental vote, and he gives them what they want, after he takes what he wants first. You know what he's pushing these days?"

Garrett just shook his head.

"He wants to buy some land to make a wildlife corridor. I got nothing against that idea. If we keep paving Florida, there won't be any wild land left except for a few parks here and there. Swain wants to buy land to connect the parks we got, so that the animals can have more space to roam. Makes sense to me. But do you know how he wants to pay for those corridors?"

Garrett shook his head again.

"Property taxes. He wants me to pay more taxes on property that I can't use."

He pushed away from the balcony railing and headed back inside. "I think I need a little more of Swain's free beer."

Garrett circled McGilray's Hole. It was gorgeous, but it had hardly been treated like the prized possession of a sincere environmentalist. The rampant vegetation that should have lined its banks was gone. Unless Garrett missed his guess, Swain kept the larger plants knocked back with herbicide, then fertilized the swathe of green lawn that set off the spring's blue-green glow so perfectly.

Swain had no choice but to fertilize. The natural soil around the spring was almost pure sand; it could never support the kind of grass Americans liked to walk on. The excess nutrients in the fertilizer obviously washed into the water. Where else could they go? Garrett thought about the downstream damage to the river caused by, year after year, pouring chemicals into water where they didn't need to be.

He had no sense that the other guests noticed their host's attack on the environment that he loved so loudly, but Garrett's job made him sensitive to such things. It was impossible to work for Florida's Department of Environmental Protection without being acutely aware of all the ways humans could spoil the landscape that had attracted them to Florida in the first place.

He was tempted to stroll up to Congressman Swain and ask, "If you can spray poison anywhere you like, how come Wynnda can't have an air conditioner?" Not being the type to cause trouble, he decided to take a walk instead. He was ready to escape Joseph Swain's well-manicured version of nature, so that he could spend some time soaking up the real thing.

The real Florida wasn't far away. Before long, Garrett was picking his way down a lightly traveled trail that led from the sandy uplands down into the surrounding marsh. Waist-high maidencane brushed against him on both sides. He wished for his snake leggings, but they weren't ordinary party attire, so he'd left them at home. When the land turned liquid beneath his boots and the swamp tupelo reached up high enough to shade out a portion of the late summer sun, he made himself a bet. If any of Congressman Swain's guests had ever left a party and ventured this far into Florida's more inhospitable territory, then he would, by God, eat those ancient leather snake leggings.

Garrett was never so at home as when he was deep in a swamp full of snakes and reptiles that would like to kill him. He could think of nothing that would lure him back to the den of human treachery at Swain's party...nothing but the double gunshot that split the humid summer air.

The bark of two nearly simultaneous shots sounded wrong. Not being a gun person, Garrett had only television shootings to go by, but he didn't think he'd ever heard a television star squeeze off just two rounds on an automatic weapon. If forced to guess, he would have said that this sounded like two people firing at almost the same time—like a shootout at the OK Corral. More likely, he'd heard two hunters trying to fell the same deer. This sounded like bad manners to Garrett, who had never hunted in his life. Wouldn't they have had some agreement beforehand on who took the shot? Otherwise, how would they know who bagged the trophy?

Garrett had no doubt that hunters prowled the woods in these parts, in and out of season, but the shots sounded way too close. Hunters had ears like rabbits. They would have heard the twanging music and the rumble of the crowd. There was plenty of wilderness around here where people weren't. Hunters would have steered clear.

Wishing harder for his snake leggings, Garrett struck out through the marsh in the direction where he thought he'd heard the shots. Within minutes, he had reached the bank of a large creek. Judging by the direction of its flow, he guessed that it was a tributary of the river that fed the wetlands stretching in every direction, as far as he could see. He imagined that the creek had once been a meandering rill, nourishing vegetation on its banks and along its bottom. It had once birthed damsel flies and apple snails and plump silvery fish, but not any more. It had been raped.

Dredges had gouged out its bottom and bitten into its banks, ripping away the natural meanders into a straight and muddy channel. Two large power boats were moored at a floating dock. A gas tank was bolted to the dock, and its nozzle was hemorrhaging fuel, one drop at a time. The setting sun lit up a rainbow slick that lay atop the water in a broad circle centered on the tank and its nozzle. There had been no attempt to hide the brown and withered weeds along the water's edge. Someone had sprayed herbicide along both banks, with gusto.

Garrett wished for a camera. He would have to report this flagrant violation of environmental law. It was his job and, what was more, he would have reported it even if it weren't, simply as an enraged citizen.

Upstream, above the point where the environmental carnage ended and nature's creekside weeds began, sat a small man holding a long cane fishing pole.

"Did you hear those shots?" he called to the fisherman, choking back the question he truly wanted to ask. *Did you do this? Why would you murder this slice of creation?*

"Hunters," the man said, reaching down and lifting a stringer of fish out of the water. "Most of them's got good enough sense to stay clear of people, but not all."

The fisherman's frayed clothing and patched boots told Garrett that he didn't own the power boats or the dock where they were moored. There was no other, more modest, boat in sight, and there was no other way to reach this spot, but Garrett knew that Stan Marquez had told the truth. Swain's house was the only one for miles around. Well, it was the only one built with a legal permit. So where had this guy come from?

"My name's Garrett Levy," he said, putting out a hand. "Do you live around here?"

The other man stuck out the hand that wasn't holding the pole and the stringer. "Frank McGilray. And, yes, I do live around here." He lifted his catch for Garrett to see. "I got carried away and caught way more fish than I can eat before they rot. I'll clean 'em and cook 'em, if you'll help me eat 'em."

Garrett took a split-second longer to respond than was strictly polite. He was assessing the cleanliness of the water where the fish were caught, which wasn't bad, as opposed to the cesspool a few dozen yards downstream. He decided that no self-respecting fish who had a choice would spend time in water that bad, so these were perfectly edible. Probably.

"I'd love to."

He followed Frank down a path that ended at a small clearing. There stood a tiny cabin inhabiting fewer square feet than the extensive vegetable garden beside it. The cabin had to be a hundred or more years old, and so did the outhouse behind it. Frank McGilray would have enjoyed a composting toilet in a way that Wynnda Swain couldn't. Such things depending on one's point of view.

This cabin's roof had no solar panels like the ones that powered Swain's naturalist fantasy. There was no glass in its windows to divide its inhabitant from nature, just rusted and patched screens. Garrett had amused himself many times by imagining a life this close to the land, but he knew he wasn't tough enough to live it. Five minutes ago, he would have said that no American was tough enough, not any more. Apparently, he was wrong.

❖ ◆ ❖ ◆ ❖

The fried fish had been delicious. The homebrewed whiskey, while not delicious, had gone a long way toward explaining why Frank's corn patch was so darn big. Garrett consumed nearly a tumblerful of the stuff before he got the nerve to ask the question that had been bugging him for hours.

"You don't seem like the creek-dredging type, Frank. And I've watched you swat mosquitoes since sundown. If bug spray's not your thing, then I don't think it was you who doused the whole countryside with weedkiller."

Frank upended his own tumbler. "It all started when Swain got attacked by a bull gator."

"How come he's still alive?"

"A smart man don't walk through these swamps unarmed. Being smarter than Swain, I shot the gator. Swain lost a hunk of meat out of his thigh, but he healed."

"When was this?"

"About ten years after he bought this property from me. I enjoyed that first ten years, and I think he did, too. He hired me to stay on as a caretaker, since he couldn't live out here, not and keep his job. All the week, he'd work in town being a lawyer, so he could afford to come out here on the weekends. This land is the only place he's happy, I'd say. He'd tie his boat up, throw his sleeping bag on the floor right there, then we'd get to work building his house. Took us a lot of years. When he was done with it, our friendship was done, too."

Garrett looked around the cabin. There were gaps in the walls big enough to let in the most monstrous palmetto bugs. The whole room smelled like Frank, and Frank smelled like a man who'd never had running water in his life. It was a warm, earthy smell that wafted out of him as if it were embedded into his skin, and Garrett liked it, in a weird sort of way. It was real. Swain had been comfortable with this cabin and its funk for years. Why did he suddenly start trying to tame the wilderness?

A vision of the denuded and maimed creek rose in front of his moonshine-addled eyes. "The gators. He's destroying their habitat so that they'll stay away."

"He wasn't about to leave his own private paradise. What else was he going to do?"

Garrett thought of the alligators of Florida, lurking like black, lumpy logs in every wet patch they could find. Trying to drive every last one of them out of any swamp was an act of supreme hubris, but then, Swain was a politician, wasn't he? Hubris was his birthright.

"What about you, Frank? You watched the alligator attack Swain. Do gators scare you now, the way they scare him?"

"They don't bother me none. I think they kinda like me. When I wade out in the water, they swim over toward me a little ways, then they stop. It's like they want to visit. Maybe they like my smell."

Garrett had heard of stranger things.

At daybreak, Garrett found that Frank's homemade whiskey didn't just taste like jet fuel—it left behind a hangover with the power of a just-lit afterburner. He was lying, fully clothed, on the hand-hewn planks of Frank's cabin floor, wanting only one thing...to go home.

He could do it, too. Too cautious to commit to an entire weekend of open-air partying, he had brought his own boat, instead of relying on Swain's flotilla of pontoon boats. It was moored to the expansive dock that stretched along the riverfront boundary of the congressman's land. The hangover might force him to ooze on his belly like a snake through the marshlands that separated him from Swain's house and the river beyond, but Garrett was pretty sure he could slither to his boat. He wanted to go home bad.

Using the kitchen table to pull himself to his feet, Garrett found that he could actually walk. Frank was passed out on the couch, so he grunted politely in his host's direction and staggered out the door and through the marsh.

He found Swain's house awash in sleeping people. There were sleeping bags thrown willy-nilly across the decks and the porches and the balconies, and all of them were occupied. Hammocks hung from trees, and tents had been pitched beneath the encircling trees. Portable toilets were scattered here and there to supplement the house's composting toilets.

Garrett was seized with the desire to see McGilray's Hole one more time, now that he'd partied with McGilray's descendant and heir. He walked through neatly trimmed greenery to the water's edge and stared down deep into the spring's cold blue depths. A massive alligator swam down toward the chasm that disgorged all that water, day in and day out.

Clamped in the gator's jaws was a man with a gleaming shock of white hair.

The only vestige remaining of Garrett's hangover was the nausea, and there could have been other explanations for that. Perhaps it stemmed from the exertion of racing to the house to wake the scuba divers who might stand a chance of saving Joseph Swain. Would they have brought spear guns with them? Could you bring a twelve-foot gator down with a spear gun? Garrett didn't know.

Deep down, he knew that these were empty questions. Every Floridian knew that gators liked to drag their living victims into the depths, roll them over and over, then wedge them under something that would keep them underwater until their dead body ripened to reptilian tastes. So perhaps Swain could have been saved when the gator first grabbed him, but not now. No living man would have hung so passively from those powerful jaws, arms and legs trailing through the water like eelgrass.

Perhaps the nausea stemmed from his single glimpse of Wynnda Swain's haunted face as she raced to the water's edge, clad in an incongruously delicate nightgown the same shade of silken gold as her toenails.

Or perhaps his stomach continued to heave because of the role he'd played in fetching Swain's body. The scuba divers had donned their gear lightning-fast, but Frank McGilray had been faster. Alerted by Swain's screaming guests, Frank had traveled the trail from his house at a dead run. He had pitched a weathered rifle at Garrett, bellowing, "If the gator surfaces, shoot him." Then Frank dove into the depths of McGilray's hole with a smooth grace that left Garrett confident that he could shoot the gator if need be.

As Frank swooped down through the water, the gator's jaws loosened and Swain floated free of its wicked teeth. The beast backed away, deliberately but steadily, giving Frank space to grab the dead man and head for the surface. When Frank's head broke the water, Garrett threw the gun aside and helped haul the men, one living and one dead, onto dry land.

Swain's body, sprawled on the spring's bank, looked... wrong. There was very little blood staining the puncture holes in his shirt, and there were few other obvious wounds, except for a grievous injury to his head.

Would a gator's teeth have done that kind of damage? There was a single hole in Swain's left temple, but the right side of his head was effectively gone. Garrett was no expert, but he would have guessed that the man was shot.

Stan Marquez was standing beside Swain's shoulder, staring down at his busted skull with the intense concentration of a man doing calculus in his head. Garrett remembered that Marquez was a hunter. He had no doubt seen what bullets could do to animals. He'd surely recognize a gunshot wound when he saw one.

Garrett took a breath, ready to cry out, "Did anybody besides me hear shots last night about sundown?", but he stifled the question. If Swain had indeed been shot, the odds were good that there was a killer among them.

Questions boiled out of the crowd. "Who saw him last?" and "Can anybody tell if he's been dead long?" and "Who's going to call the sheriff?"

Garrett had been to campouts like this one before. At sundown, people withdrew to their tents and hammocks. Guitars and banjos came out. So did liquor bottles. Partiers sat huddled around bonfires and camp lanterns in clusters of four or five or seven. It was absolutely possible that Swain could have been gone without being missed since sunset...since those gunshots sounded.

The only discordant note in that theory was Wynnda. She would have known that he didn't sleep in their bedroom. Wouldn't she have gone looking for him? Ordinarily, yes, any woman would worry if her husband didn't come to bed. Unless she was accustomed to it.

Garrett cried out, "I'll call nine-one-one," fetching his cell phone out of his pocket. Glad to have an excuse to back away from all the people and find a quiet place, he ducked behind the house and called the emergency personnel. When the dispatcher heard where Garrett was, she let out a little puff of breath. "It'll take at least an hour to get somebody to you, maybe a lot more. Do you want me to stay on the line?"

"No. But you better send the sheriff along with the paramedics. Some of us think it was murder."

Garrett was surprised at his need—no, his deep-seated drive—to find out who killed Joseph Swain. He hadn't known the man, and he hadn't liked what he'd seen of him, but his sense of justice was strong and it had been offended today, as surely as it had been offended by the environmental murder of the little creek that he'd seen the day before.

And perhaps his sense that this death was a puzzle to be unraveled, like a knotty thermodynamics problem, was rooted in his engineering training. If his suspicions were correct, Swain had been dead all night. The evidence was deteriorating, fading into the marsh as each second passed. Spatters of blood were being consumed by insects. Spongy soil was springing back into shape, obscuring footprints. Each tick of the clock gave the killer time to obliterate any traces left behind. Justice couldn't wait for an hour.

If Swain had been killed when those shots sounded at dusk, then he had been deep in the marsh. Garrett bolted in that direction, intent on finding the spot where the congressman had died. It must have been somewhere near the creek where he'd met Frank. He stumbled when he realized what that meant. Frank could have been Swain's killer.

Garrett reasoned that Frank couldn't be eliminated as a suspect—nobody could at this point—but his gut said the man was innocent, for two reasons. First, Frank had had countless opportunities to kill Swain and he would have countless more. They were routinely alone together in the deep wilderness. Under those conditions, Frank could have had every expectation of getting away with murder. Why should he kill Swain now, with a hundred witnesses nearby?

What was more, Garrett had seen Frank's face when he pulled his longtime friend out of the water. There had been a tenderness there, a grief more heartfelt than even Swain's wife showed.

Which begged the question of whether Wynnda Swain might have pulled the trigger on her husband. Her unhappiness was palpable. Murder was certainly not the only option in escaping a bad marriage, but Garrett had friends who had been divorced from lawyers. The results were never pretty.

"Hey, Garrett! Hold up!"

Stan Marquez rushed toward him. The cast on his leg flashed white against the rank undergrowth hampering his progress. His injured leg gave him a lopsided, galloping gait, but it didn't seem to slow him down. Garrett realized that his subconscious had been considering and casting aside suspects, while his conscious mind focused on which soggy bit of land was most likely to support his next step. He hadn't considered Stan, because he'd doubted that the man could have hobbled out to the murder site. Perhaps he'd been wrong.

Stan was a hunter. He knew how to use a gun. He knew how to get around in the swamp. He had ample reason to hate Swain. And he was running headlong toward Garrett.

A cold sweat prickled Garrett's backbone. He'd been treating the situation like a problem with a solution that could be neatly calculated. Now he might be alone in the wilderness with a hunter whose freshest kill was human.

Stan was twenty feet away and moving fast, until his bad leg went down ankle-deep in a mudhole.

"Damn. My doctor's going to kill me. My wife, too."

The cast. It had been clean when Garrett first spotted Stan, and he'd watched it grow progressively dirtier with every step. It would have been impossible for the man to have hiked out to the creek, shot Swain, and returned to the party without completely trashing the white plaster cast. Stan didn't kill the congressman.

"Wait, Stan. If you come any further, the mud'll suck that thing off your leg altogether."

The big man stood still. "But you need help. I'd bet money that Swain wasn't killed by any gator. Somebody shot his head nearly off. I heard shots late yesterday and, judging by the direction you're headed, I think you did, too. Nobody at the party paid much attention, figuring it was hunters, but I wondered. I can't let you go out there alone."

"I'll be okay. The killer won't be standing on the spot where he killed Swain, waiting for me. But you can help. Go back to the party and look for tracks. The soil around McGilray's Hole is light and sandy, but the rest of the dirt around here is black muck like this." He gestured at the heavy mud coating their boots. "If you see mud anywhere near the house, we'll want to know who tracked it back to the party. Check the decks, especially. This kind of muck will be obvious on the bare wood."

He tried to think like someone with something major to hide.

"Look on the banks around the spring and along the river, too. You could rinse off the top layer of mud by just wading in the water, but it would take soap and a scrub brush to get really clean. So check everybody's feet."

"Only a nut would go wading around here after dark. That's when the gators come out."

"True, but check anyway. And check the dock and the boats. See if it looks like somebody cleaned up out there. They would have needed to stash their dirty clothes somewhere, and the river's spring-fed, so it's too clear for them to sink the evidence."

Stan looked pensive. "The killer's in a real hole. The only safe place around here to hide dirty clothes and boots is in the swamp—and he'll get muddy again, trying to get out of the swamp."

"Or she," Garrett said, thinking of Wynnda. "I'll take the house. I'll need to check the bathrooms for—"

"Bathtub rings. Dirty towels. Stuff like that."

"Exactly."

❖ ◆ ❖ ◆ ❖

The spot where Swain died hadn't proven hard to find. He'd left a trail behind him. Blood and tissue had spattered onto a nearby tree. And the broad, wallowed-out trail of a gator led toward the nearby creek.

The site told him nothing about who killed Swain or why, but it might reveal far more to forensics experts. Garrett stayed well clear, doing his best to avoid contaminating any evidence. At least he'd be able to get the investigators here quickly. He headed back to the house, hoping to uncover something that would point to the guilty party.

The yard around Swain's house was filled with people who had clean feet. The porches and stairs and decks were tracked with only grass and sand. The floors inside were clean, because Swain's guests were well-brought-up. They wiped their feet on the doormats provided. The doormats were free of mud, until Garrett wiped his own mucky feet on them.

Stan rushed up and whispered, "The dock was clean. So were the boats."

Garrett thanked him and continued his methodical search of the house. The bathrooms were as clean as could be expected, considering that a hundred people had been present for twenty hours.

The composting toilet offered an interesting twist for an amateur detective. An ordinary toilet might have concealed some evidence of a killer cleaning up evidence. A dirty washrag could be flushed. Even muddy socks could go down the sewage pipes, one at a time. A composting toilet, on the other hand, stored waste in a holding tank, until it was treated and ready for removal. A dirty washrag and a pair of socks could be waiting in one of the toilets' tanks, but Garrett considered retrieving them a job for the police.

Single-minded in his search, he burst into the master bedroom, only to find Wynnda standing at the window, weeping. She was still wrapped in the gold silk she'd slept in, and she still looked as out-of-place as a porcelain doll floating in a mud puddle.

Women like Wynnda had always made Garrett feel like his voice was too loud and his feet were too big. Today, his big feet were coated in muck. "I—I was looking for a bathroom," he croaked.

She pointed with a neatly manicured hand, and he stumbled into a room where every porcelain surface gleamed. Wynnda had not scrubbed half a swamp's worth of mud off her body in here, but he'd known that as soon as he saw her. Garrett had spent a life enjoying nature, then washing it off himself when he got home. He wore high-top rubber boots when he went into wetlands. Nevertheless, when he got home, there was invariably soil ground into his heels. Muddy water always sloshed over the tops of his boots, leaving black dirt clinging to his cuticles and the rough skin on the ball of the foot.

If Wynnda had ventured out into the marsh last night to kill her husband, she could have spent the whole night with soap and a scrub brush and nail polish remover and cuticle moisturizer, but the creamy skin on her feet would still not have the flawless sheen he'd just observed.

Garrett backed out of the widow's marriage chamber, mumbling apologies. There was only one person whose feet were dirty enough to be the killer of Wynnda's husband. Remembering the double-shot he'd heard, Garrett finally realized why Swain had been killed, and that motive affected him so personally that he had no choice but to confront the killer. And he felt reasonably sure that he'd be safe in doing so.

❖ ◆ ❖ ◆ ❖

Frank sat in the spot where Garrett first saw him. Raising a hand in greeting, he said, "I've been waiting for you. I knew you'd figure it out, and I wanted to say good-bye."

"You saved my life."

"I loved Swain in my own way, even after he raped my land and killed my creek, but I couldn't let him shoot you. It was so hard to pull that trigger on my friend that I was almost too late. My bullet caught him just as he fired on you but, thank God, his shot went wild. Do you understand why he wanted you dead?"

"He knew I worked for the state environmental agency, and he knew what would happen if I saw what he'd done to the creek. That's the worst case of illegal dredging I've ever seen. The agency would have hauled him into court. The fines and the cost of restoration would have been astronomical. More to the point, his political career would have been in the toilet. Has he carried a gun ever since the alligator attack?"

"Yep. And I always have. Cottonmouths in these parts are worse than gators. When I saw him draw a bead on an unarmed man, I had no choice but to drop him. You'd have done the same."

The part of him that abhorred guns and what they did to people said, "No," but the part of him that craved justice nodded in agreement.

"I wish I didn't try to hide it yesterday, though," Frank went on. "I should have told you what I'd done, soon as I saw you. Instead, I left him laying there, because I was scared. Then I took you back to my house so you wouldn't stumble on the body. When it got light, I left you drunk on the floor and went looking for Swain, so's I could bury him, but he was gone. For a gator to get him, even after he was dead...well, that's the worst thing he could have imagined. I didn't wish that on him."

"What will you do now, Frank? The sheriff will be here any minute."

"I won't be here when he comes. Nobody but you and Wynnda know I was ever here, and she won't talk. Many's the time Swain brought her out here, then took off in his speedboat to enjoy nature and shoot a few gators. Wynnda needs someone to talk to, and sometimes I was all she had. You might think about telling her what happened. 'Course, if you tell the sheriff, I guess she'll find out from him. It's your call."

Frank eased himself down into the creek and started wading upstream, away from the carnage left by Swain's dredges and herbicides and into the fresh clear water where sunfish and alligators lived.

"The sheriff will find your house," Garrett called after him. "They'll be looking for you."

"Swain's held title to my house and property for more'n thirty years. He promised to let me live on it for life, which he did, and he promised to take care of it, which he didn't. Here's what I figure," he said, looking over his shoulder. "The sheriff will see that my cabin's been lived in, and he'll figure a bum's been squatting there. Maybe he'll figure the bum killed Swain, but that's as far as he'll ever get."

"Everybody saw you haul Swain out of the water."

"Did they get my name? Does anybody but you and Wynnda know it? Anyhow, the sheriff can't track me out here, so go ahead and tell him what you know, if it'll make you feel better. I got no reason to ever set foot in civilization again. I'm not a hundred percent sure I've even got a birth certificate, so who's he gonna look for? I hear that smart folks like you have just about paved all of Florida, but there's enough land like this left where I can live just fine."

Frank was hip-deep in the creek, so he was leaving neither footprints that a man could track nor a trail that a dog could follow. A gator slid on its belly into the water and swam in Frank's direction, following him at a respectful distance.

"If you decide not to turn me in, take the whiskey jug out of the cabinet and put it on the table. I'll come back in a while and see whether you did. I'd like to live out my days here, where my daddy and granddaddy were born and died. If that jug's on the table, I'll know I can."

"But you killed him to save me. Why don't you just stay and explain things to the sheriff?"

Frank's laugh echoed on the water. "Look at me. I'm dirty. I smell. I killed a rich politician. If they catch me, they'll put me under the jail. I'll take my chances out here with the gators." As if called, a second gator eased into the water, following Frank upstream. The reptilian form of its long leathery body reflected in the calm water, doubling its primeval power.

Later, when the sheriff and his people had come and gone, Garrett knew he would ask Wynnda if she'd like to help him leave the moonshine jug out for Frank.

I got an email shortly after I submitted "Land of the Flowers" to my editor, Claudia Bishop, apologizing for something she didn't do. Or rather, apologizing for something that she almost did.

Claudia, who winters in Florida and should know better, had been poised to take me to task over the dead-body-in-the-gator's-mouth scene. She had thought it was implausi-

ble. Then, after she read the story and before she called me up and told me that I'd gone over the top, there were three gator attacks in Florida in about a week. Those poor people's grisly ends were plastered all over the news, forcing her to rethink her position.

Floridians know that alligators are lurking in or near practically every wet spot in the state. It is far safer to bet on the presence of a gator than on its absence. We also know that, on the whole, they tend to leave people alone. Small dogs are much easier to eat, which is why so many dead gators are found to have a collection of collars and rabies tags in their stomachs.

Humans who find themselves tangling with gators are usually humans who found themselves in the wrong place at the wrong time. Sometimes, it's just the luck of the draw. You can't blame a swimmer who runs and jumps into a lake for the ten thousandth time and is just unlucky enough to land on an alligator this time. (You can't blame the gator for biting him, either.)

Other times, you just have to wonder what the victim was thinking. Going swimming in a canal at sundown (feeding time) and taking your toy poodle (gator bait) with you could be interpreted as asking for trouble, if the interpreter were an unsympathetic soul. In the case of the victim in "Land of the Flowers," I don't know that he was asking for gator trouble. But I do think he might have needed killing, and the gators brought him their own brand of justice.

May he rest in peace.

– Mary Anna

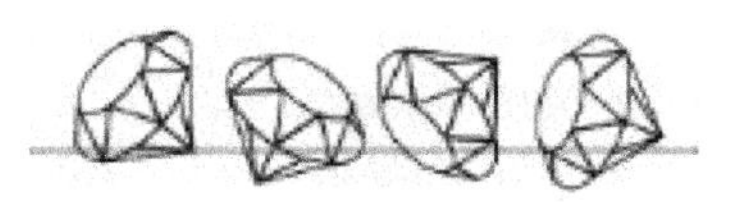

TWIN SET

Sometimes, it only takes a single nugget of information to trigger a story, or even a book. In the case of "Twin Set," I saw a television detective explain that DNA samples taken from identical twins are indistinguishable to a crime lab. This information sent me straight to the internet. I don't remember which fictional detective gave me this information, so let's just dig around in the past for the TV Land metaphor I'm about to deliver: Just because Matlock says something on television doesn't make it true. (And just because it's on the internet doesn't make it true, either, but I do try to be savvy about which websites I believe.)

The internet confirmed the detective's statement. (Within reason...there were various caveats like "If one twin had a significant mutation after birth and if it was easily detectable on the chunk of DNA we were testing, then yeah, maybe we could tell 'em apart.")

Mystery writers have to be capable of dipping into the icky, slimy brain of a killer, even if (like me) they personally couldn't kill anything, not even if a horde of rabid squirrels was advancing on them with foamy, dripping jaws. So I dipped into the brain of a person with murderous intent, who just happened to be an identical twin.

If that person had been watching the very same program I'd just seen, what might that person do? And what would happen to the poor victimized twin, the one who was framed for murder? When I bashed those questions up against the complicated emotional relationship that would have to exist between two brilliant and beautiful women who had been in head-to-head competition since the moment of their birth, I knew I had my story.

– Mary Anna

TWIN SET

I am not my sister.

Bailey's shadow fell over my life less than a minute after I was born, when she shoved her way out of our mother's womb. The doctor laid me down—tenderly, I'm sure—to look after her more pressing needs. Once Bailey's airway was cleared, her oxygen-starved complexion shifted from death's-door blue to baby-girl pink, and our pediatrician became the first to utter the refrain that has haunted us for thirty years now: "I don't think I've ever seen a pair of twins who are so absolutely identical. They're mirror images of each other." At least, that's how our mother always told the story.

In the meantime, I waited—quietly, according to Mother—until all of Bailey's needs were met. Then someone found the time to wipe the birth blood off me and welcome me to the world.

Having begun my life smeared in blood, perhaps I shouldn't have been surprised when I woke up half an hour ago, covered in a sheet heavy with the stuff. Perhaps it would have been better if the blood were mine.

It was the movie that triggered the attack. There can't be any doubt. Hardly a week ago, I lay curled in that self-same bed beside Mack, watching a movie about a twin who committed a murder and tried to pin the crime on his brother. The handsome investigator was stumped because DNA testing can't distinguish between samples collected from identical twins. Or identical triplets or quadruplets, for that matter. Even if one twin's DNA mutates after conception, the difference is usually undetectable by forensics labs.

I was troubled by the knowledge that my sister might also be absorbing this dangerous information, so troubled that I lied to Mack. I told him I needed to run next door to Bailey's apartment to retrieve a sweater, or I'd have nothing to wear to work the next day.

"You girls should just knock down the wall between your closets. I don't think either of you ever wears your own stuff," Mack had said, reaching his long arms overhead and stretching every muscle on a body that was well-blessed with them.

Mack was half right. I never wore my own stuff, because Bailey's closet was always full of my clothes and hers, too.

I let myself into her apartment without knocking and found her watching political commentary on PBS, but it was an obvious ploy. I sensed that she had anticipated my arrival and changed the channel, and Mack's death proves that my intuition was right. Twins know each other in ways that are somehow more than natural, but still not supernatural.

How else can I explain what has happened? Seven days ago, the television detective told me that Bailey and I are indistinguishable to a crime lab, and now Mack is dead.

❖ ◆ ❖ ◆ ❖

"Fingerprints," the handsome television detective had observed, "are formed after conception, in the womb. They are truly individual. Even identical twins have unique fingerprints."

Too bad Bailey is so careful to bleach her hair to the exact shade of platinum that I prefer. This means that both of our bathroom closets are equally well-stocked with rubber gloves. They do a great job of protecting our hands from peroxide. It is highly unlikely that she would have been barehanded when she slipped into my apartment, slid my chef's knife out of a kitchen drawer, and slid it through Mack's ribs into his heart. Several times.

I should have seen this coming. Our history is littered with stolen boyfriends and headless dolls. And now Mack is the latest casualty of our lifelong battles. Not that he was left headless, like our entire flock of childhood Barbies. His gentle face was spared but, judging from the condition of my sheets, I would guess that he was left bloodless, or nearly so.

I don't know how long I lay there in my defiled bed, asking, "How could I have been here, six inches away from Mack, while this happened? How did Bailey accomplish this?"

My neurons didn't seem to be firing properly, a problem that was both the answer to my question and the reason I was so slow to recognize that answer.

When had I been drugged?

The three of us had sipped martinis on the balcony just before midnight, then Bailey had gone home. The digital clock on my nightstand told me that it was now nearly four.

Who had poured those martinis? It didn't matter. It would have been no trick for a treacherous sister to slip a bitter powder into a bitter drink.

And into Mack's drink, too? God, I hoped so. When I emerged from the drug and from the shock, it was going to help me if I could convince myself that he didn't suffer.

I raked my eyes over the bedroom, dimly illuminated by the muted television and the face of my alarm clock. Had she left a trace of herself behind, something that would convince a jury when I told them she'd done this? The prospect of Bailey in prison made me catch my breath. All my life, I'd dreamed of being free of her, and now that dream was in reach.

I huddled in the bed for a sick moment, trying to think. My entire apartment was a crime scene. What if I set my bloodied foot on the carpet and obliterated the only shred of evidence that would put Bailey away? What if I reached out my hand and picked up the phone, dialed 911, and in the process lost my chance to have her locked up? Prudence suggested that I take a moment to look around.

A faint sheen of streetlamp glow penetrated the French doors that opened onto my balcony—the balcony where we had lingered so pleasantly, four hours before. A nightlight in the kitchen leaked brightness through the cracks around my bedroom door. Bailey had been in my kitchen, too, before our final cocktail hour. And she'd lain sprawled across our bed, watching the weather forecast, just before she left for the night.

Her fingerprints were everywhere in my apartment. Her hair, too, was everywhere: in the bed where I slept, in my clothes, on the floor, in my dryer's lint trap. Not that it mattered, unless a forensics lab had developed some secret way of discerning my hair, grown by the same DNA and colored by the same dye, from hers.

The chef's knife lay beside me, atop a thick comforter that had been snowy white just a few hours before. I didn't need any special fingerprint powder to know that the only prints on it were mine, not when Bailey had a full stock of rubber gloves in her bathroom. I studied the knife lying mere inches from my right hand and asked myself how I could possibly prove to a jury that it wasn't me who opened my lover's chest and let him die?

The answer was clear. I couldn't prove it, not with mere science. Before I involved the police, Bailey and I were going to work this little problem out.

Sister to sister.

❖ ◆ ❖ ◆ ❖

Why did Bailey and I live in the same apartment building, work in the same industry, and run with the same crowd of friends when we detested each other so? Out of sheer force of habit? No. But not out of love, either.

In our crib—no, in our mother's womb—we learned the importance of keeping an eye on one's enemy. All these years, whether we were grappling over a picture book or a tube of lipstick or a man, we've always remained face-to-face. For thirty years, I have stared in horror at my own face in the mirror.

I have known twins who carried lifelong scars because they weren't considered "the smart one" or "the athletic one" or "the pretty one." Bailey and I never suffered from those labels. Is either of us prettier? I can't give an unbiased opinion on that, but men seem to like us both. Neither of us is athletic, and both of us are smart. Even in high school, it is difficult to feel a sense of competition with your sister when both of you scored a hundred percent on yesterday's algebra test.

If we'd been different people, the experience might have bonded us. It can be lonely when you're surrounded by people who can't grasp the concept that *x* sometimes equals two and it sometimes equals seventy-two. Everybody in ninth grade was floored by the notion that you couldn't just nail down a value for *x* once and get it over with. Everybody, that is, but Bailey and me, but we hated each other for reasons that had nothing to do with algebra, so we didn't bond. We just lived our lonely lives, side by side.

If our enmity didn't arise out of jealousy or competition, then where did it come from? I can't speak for most other people, but I can speak for Bailey because I've watched every minute of her life. I know her. I'm not her, but I am, in some weird way. Both of us are suffused with the bone-deep knowledge that the other sister just shouldn't be there. Each of us has been cursed with the ultimate intruder.

Why did Bailey kill Mack? Because he made me happy? Or because she saw him first? Men have a habit of seeing Bailey first, then recognizing her for what she is and turning to me, but she never killed any of the others. Why Mack, and why now? Maybe because we're thirty now and, soon enough, men will stop seeing her first. Before long, they'll stop seeing either of us at all. What will it be like to look in the mirror and find that we've become invisible?

Having already determined that the legal system was not going to save me from Bailey, I decided to save myself. I stretched my right hand toward the knife and wrapped my fingers around its handle. It balanced easily in my hand, as well it should, considering how much it had cost me. Its blade was forged of high carbon steel, which the saleswoman had said maintained the sharpest edge, and it was of full tang construction, which she had told me was the strongest design.

Bailey's evening activities had rendered the woman's sales pitch a trifle macabre.

Knife in hand, I rose from the bed. Within a few staggering steps, I had regained most of the equilibrium that the drug had stolen. Piled on the floor outside the bedroom door, I found a sweater, a pair of jeans, some socks, and a pair of loafers. They were all soaked in blood, and they were all mine. It appeared that Bailey had returned some of the clothes she borrowed. If she was smart—and she was—she'd probably showered in my bathroom and departed in some of the clean clothes that I'd left folded atop my dryer.

I lifted the key to Bailey's apartment from its hook beside the refrigerator. Then, key in one hand and killer blade in the other, I left Mack behind and went looking for my sister.

Bailey's apartment was immediately adjacent to mine, which means that our front doors were hardly twenty feet apart. That's not very far, but it was a long way to walk in my bloody negligée.

There was little chance of my being seen at this unholy hour. Had anyone seen Bailey creep in the other direction a few hours before, then back home? Even if they had, their testimony wouldn't help me defend myself against an accusation that I murdered Mack. The differences between us were so subtle—hair that whorled in opposite directions on the back of our skulls, mirror-image birthmarks on our shoulders—that the casual observer would have merely assumed that I was walking into my own apartment.

Bailey had committed the perfect crime, but she never reckoned that I would rise up against her. That I would finally say, "I refuse to take this any more. No matter what the consequence." She didn't take into consideration that framing me for murder left me with very little to lose.

I was glad that Bailey's apartment was to the left of mine, so that I could trail my left hand along the wall to steady myself as I walked down the corridor. My body would eventually win its war with adrenaline and the remnants of knockout drops, but I was not enjoying my time in the battlefield. The key in my hand raked lightly across the textured wallpaper and the sound rubbed like sandpaper against my eardrums. I regretted smudging blood on the expensive wallpaper, but it couldn't be helped. Neither could the crimson smears my feet left on the carpet. They stretched behind me like the tracks of a frostbitten woman lost in the snow.

As my mind shook off the chemicals, flashes of memory began to plague me. A sharp shadow on the wall. The weak sheen of moonlight on steel. Blood that flowed black in my darkened room.

These visions rocked my tentative equilibrium, threatening to knock me off my feet. They gave me the strength to press on.

I groped my way to my sister's doorknob and turned the key.

❖ ◆ ❖ ◆ ❖

I could tell by the bags under Bailey's eyes that she had been asleep, but we're all programmed to wake at the sound of an unexpected key in the front door. She stepped into the living room as I rushed headlong through her apartment, and I was disappointed. Her bedroom was identical to the one where Mack lay dead, and I had so wanted to confront her there.

She stood swaying in her powder-pink nightgown, and matching satin slippers peeked from beneath its hem. We have always looked particularly nice in that color. Her eyes were so dilated that I could hardly make out their deep blue irises. It occurred to me that, in a stroke of genius, she'd gone home after Mack was dead and drugged herself, making it look as though I were the one doing the drugging and the killing.

She clutched her phone. Had she planned to greet a burglar politely, then call the police? "What have you done, Haley? Are you hurt?" she asked, as if I were the one who had brought this calamity down on both our heads. "Does Mack know where you are?"

My grip tightened on the handle of the knife hidden in the folds of my nightgown, which had once been powder pink, too. "Mack is dead. You know that."

The phone clattered to the floor. Her face crumpled like it did when she was a little girl, and she was having trouble getting her way.

"You didn't have to do that. He was never coming back to me." She put both hands to her face. "You can finally quit torturing me now, because I'll suffer over this for the rest of my life."

"Don't worry," I said, as the knife rose high over my head and I thought of Mack. "You won't suffer for long."

Her left arm shot up and her forearm caught my descending wrist, deflecting the blow. She used her right hand to pull me toward her, destroying the leverage that I would need to use the knife effectively.

"You're slow, Haley." Her lips, just like my lips, were inches from my face. "I feel like I've been drugged, but you're even slower than I am. Did you drug yourself, too, so you could pretend you were unconscious when someone killed Mack?" Her eyes widened and I could see their pink rims, lined with pale lashes. "Were you going to pretend that I did it?"

"*You* did it. *You*."

I bore down on her upturned arm.

Tears washed down her face. "Didn't you ever love me, Haley? Not ever?"

I shifted my weight, trying to break her hold, but she anticipated the feint and moved with me. Why would her reflexes be better than mine when we wore the same body and had lived essentially the same life? If she were right, if she had been drugged before Mack died and I'd been drugged after I...after somebody killed him, then she would be more alert than I. Her quickness, both mental and physical, suggested that she had guessed right.

In the instant that I doubted my memory, Bailey exploited her advantage. She thrust her right hand out and pushed me an arm's length away. Then she bent her yoga-conditioned knee up between her breasts, planted her foot on my chest, and pushed hard. I landed halfway across the room and could only watch, impotent, as she backed through her bedroom door and locked it. Fortunately, I lived in an identical apartment, and I knew that the flimsy little lock was mainly just for show. My own yoga-conditioned legs would make short work of it.

"The DNA lab will see us as the same person," I shouted through the door. "There's no physical evidence that will pin this on me. It'll be my word against yours, and the jury will believe me."

"People believe you. They always have." She fell silent, as if she were reviewing all the times—and there were many—that my word had prevailed over hers.

I punctuated the silence with a kick to the door.

"But, Haley, there *is* physical evidence this time, if you used that knife in your hand to kill Mack."

I answered her with another solid kick.

"We're mirror twins, Haley. You know that."

As if I could forget. Everyone who ever saw us was fascinated by the two pretty girls who could each pass for the other's reflection. Bailey's hair parted on the left, and mine parted on the right. My dimple, the one that had so charmed Mack, was in my left cheek. Bailey's was on the right. Looking at her was like looking into a cruel mirror.

"The police will be able to tell whether the killer was right-handed or left-handed. Where was Mack stabbed? On his right side, or his left?"

Through the heart. Mack had been stabbed through the heart, from the front. On his left side. This meant that his killer was right-handed. And I was the right-handed twin.

I put my shoulder to the door, shoving it over and over until the lock broke. When the door flew open, Bailey was nowhere in sight.

I hovered on the balls of my feet, searching the room's dark corners, ready to spring at a sudden movement. I saw nothing, only an unmade bed and a cluttered desk. Like my room, much of the ambient light came from the French doors that opened onto the balcony. I reached for the light switch but, having spotted my prey, I drew back my hand. It would be so much better to creep up on Bailey in the dark.

The toe of a powder pink slipper was barely visible through the bottom pane of the French door. Bailey had retreated too far, and she'd left herself no escape route. I crossed the room in four steps, flung the door open, and turned to face her.

There was no one there.

A disembodied satin slipper rested at my feet, carefully laid as a decoy. I looked over the railing, half-hoping to see her body sprawled below me, but I was disappointed.

I turned back toward the door in time to witness Bailey's treachery. A well-manicured hand reached out from beneath the bed, shoved the door closed, and shot the bolt that attached it to the floor. She scrambled from her hiding place, turned the dead bolt, and ran screaming from the room. I watched her scoop the telephone off the floor and run straight out into the hall, where I knew she would begin banging on the neighbors' doors. It's certainly what I would have done.

It would do me no good to smash the panes in the French door and go rushing after Bailey, because she had already woken a flock of witnesses. Loud voices were sounding in the hallway outside her apartment while I weighed my options. Someone would come for me soon.

My body had almost cleansed itself of the drug. Uncomfortable flashes of memory had begun to convince me that Bailey might be right about who killed Mack. I could visualize the knife swinging down in a powerful arc and striking home, over and over, and the movie scene in my mind's eye was not shot from the angle of a woman lying in bed beside the victim.

But this didn't mean that Bailey could prove it to a jury, not beyond a reasonable doubt. And it didn't mean that Bailey didn't plant awful memories in my mind when I was drugged and suggestible.

I dropped the knife into the bushes below, angling my toss so that it landed halfway between my balcony and Bailey's. That should confuse the courtroom conversation for a few days.

Perhaps the killer threw it from the balcony after killing Mack, my lawyer would say. *Perhaps my client wasn't carrying it when she came to tell Bailey that he was dead. It's always possible that Bailey was mistaken. Or that she's lying to cover the fact that she killed him herself.*

My lawyer would have to be damn good to pin this on Bailey, since Mack's wounds were obviously made by a right-handed attacker, but he could always try. *My client's sister has studied yoga for years. She could have trained her-*

self to use her right hand well enough to kill an unconscious man.

My attorney could plan for a fallback position—*Perhaps a right-handed stranger broke into my client's apartment with a knife*—but I'd really prefer to go after Bailey. Labeling her as the culprit would do a better job of explaining the drugs that will be found in all three of our systems. And seeing her accused would give me great personal satisfaction.

I knew it would take me some time to think through the details of my defense and, as I said before, I knew I would need a damn good lawyer. Unusual intelligence would be a point in my favor, though it was somewhat mitigated by the fact that my equally intelligent sister would be testifying for the other side.

I clearly had a lot to think about. I was still weighing my options when the sirens sounded on the street below.

Storytellers have loved to tell stories about twins since time began. Diana and Apollo. Jacob and Esau. Susan and Sharon in The Parent Trap. *The dramatic possibilities inherent in the twin relationship will never end.*

In "Twin Set," I wanted to deal with an aspect of the biology of twinship that no one understood for most of history, even as recently as 1961 when The Parent Trap *was filmed. Identical twins originate at conception from the same DNA, which is not something that comes into play in everyday life...not unless they are involved in a crime which requires forensic labwork. Like murder, for instance.*

After conception or, to be completely accurate, after the dividing cells split into two parts that will each develop into a separate human being, those two identical humans experience different lives. Their individual environments and experiences can provoke the development of strongly individual personalities. For example, if one twin is favored by their parents, both children will be affected, for good or ill. Perhaps this was the case with Haley and Bailey, but we don't really know, because we can't be sure we trust anything Haley says, now can we? It is just as possible that they both possessed a gene for homicidal insanity, but that some random cosmic ray tripped it in only one of them. But which one?

Even their body types can be very different, if one twin receives better nutrition or care, but this isn't the case with these beautiful and brilliant blonde twins. They are physically completely identical, except for the fluke that they are mirror twins. As I wrote the story, it occurred to me that there is a psychological element to mirror twins. When a garden-variety twin looks in the mirror, she sees someone who differs subtly from her sister. When mirror twins look at each other, they each see the person in the mirror. They see themselves. What does that do to a person's very identity?

Beyond exploring the questions of twinship, I had one more goal in writing "Twin Set." I wanted to play around with the concept of the unreliable narrator. You have just read a story from the point-of-view of someone who has been drugged unconscious. That person may or may not be sane.

What really happened to Mack? The police and the forensics team will do their best to figure it out, but will they ever be sure? More to the point...will you?

– Mary Anna

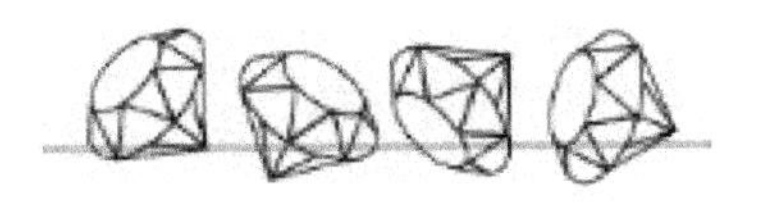

LOW-BUDGET MONSTER FLICK

Gorgeous babes in white bathing suits.

Weary young men, happy to be home from Guadalcanal and Iwo Jima.

Palm trees. Spanish moss. Glass-clear water.

Ambition. Murderous jealousy. The culture clash between Hollywood and the repressed sexuality of mid-20th century America.

Alligators.

Lots and lots of alligators....

What could possibly go wrong?

-Mary Anna

LOW-BUDGET MONSTER FLICK

In my own defense, I'll say that the job sounded good when I took it. Who wouldn't jump at the chance to get paid to spend a month in Florida doing wardrobe and makeup for the most voluptuous starlet on the silver screen, Carlotta Verona? Particularly when the wardrobe in question consists entirely of skimpy bathing suits and torn blouses ...thin, wet, torn blouses.

It was hardly a year after Hiroshima. In those days, my nightmares still inhabited the sweltering damp hellholes of the South Pacific, and those nightmares were heavily punctuated with gunfire and haunted by death. I was picturing a few healing weeks on a broad sandy beach, surrounded by bathing beauties. (Did I mention that I was to be paid for this?)

Benny Schulz neglected to mention that I'd be working in a sweltering damp swamp that looked a helluva lot like the South Pacific, if I crossed my eyes and squinted. Benny Schulz was your typical lying, cheating, stealing Hollywood assistant producer, but he was my friend. How could he have known that he was sending me to yet another steamy jungle where the nights were haunted by death?

Benny hired me for this gig because I could build a face for any monster a movie mogul could imagine. Warts, scars, scales, open oozing wounds—Benny called me whenever a director needed a glamorous movie star to be ugly. I enjoyed doing warts and scales. Scars and open oozing wounds? Not so much. They put me too much in mind of the things I saw on Guadalcanal.

So imagine how I felt when I arrived in that godforsaken swamp and saw that this movie monster didn't need my magic at all. I was so upset that I bullied the director into letting me make a long-distance call, just so I could yell at Benny.

"Dammit, they're making a movie about a rubber fish! Or lizard or turtle or...shit, Benny. I don't know what it is. It's just an ugly-looking monster with a zipper up its back. The director's gonna put an actor in this rubber suit and throw him in the water, and that's that. Instant monster."

"So what's the problem?"

"Benny. It's an allover suit...not a square inch of actor showing. Know what that means?"

"It means we can put somebody cheap in there, 'cause nobody ain't gonna see who it is?"

Cheap was good in Benny's world.

"Benny, it means there's nothing for the makeup guy to do. Meaning there's nothing for *me* to do here but spread pancake makeup on Carlotta Verona's pretty face."

"'Zat mean you get to touch her with your bare hands? 'Cause maybe you can tell her she needs a beauty mark on her chest." Benny's constant lecherous leer had seeped into his voice and was oozing out of the receiver. I had a sudden urge to go wash my ear.

"You're wasting money, Benny. I don't come cheap. You coulda hired anybody to smear lipstick around. It's not hard to make Carlotta look good."

Benny's snort communicated the pain of an assistant producer watching dollars fly out the door. "Too late now. I already paid to get you over there. I could bring you home and fly somebody cheap to Florida, but it'd cost more than I'd save." This had to be true, because Benny didn't make errors when dollar signs were involved. When Benny thought about money, you could hear the percussive thunk of an adding machine lever being pulled. "You're just gonna have to stay there and find excuses to rub your hands on Carlotta. And her stunt double, who may actually have bigger tits, if such a thing is possible."

"Does the rest of her look like Carlotta?"

"Yeah, only more so. And since Debbie ain't famous, she ain't got a rich old ugly boyfriend like Vince Carmichael chasing her around. A chump like you might have a chance with her. I think you're gonna like this job. Feel free to thank me."

I mumbled, "Thanks," and hung up, but I didn't mean it.

I looked out at an endless array of cypress trees dripping Spanish moss. They shaded an untamed river fed by Glitter Spring, a watery abyss that belched out about a trillion gallons of diamond-clear water every day. I've still never seen anything like that water. It was clear as air. You could shoot a movie through it, which is precisely why we were there.

The landscape here hadn't changed since the dinosaurs walked. I could have written a blockbuster script about those dinosaurs. People would've been tossing their popcorn sky-high in happy horror. I knew I could do it, just like all those other people in Hollywood who were damn sure they could be actors or directors or...yeah...screenwriters. It just about killed me that Benny would only hire me for making monster makeup and smearing lipstick.

There were monsters out there in Glitter Spring, but they weren't movie monsters in rubber suits. They were cold-blooded, muscle-bound killing machines covered in scaly black skin and armed with fearsome teeth. Once, after we'd finished shooting, I asked the boat captain to take me close to those natural monsters, thinking I might get makeup ideas for my next horror movie. I learned that thirty seconds spent staring into the passionless eyes of an alligator felt like thirty seconds too long.

This California boy didn't feel safe in that primeval wasteland where pterodactyls would have felt right at home. I didn't feel like thanking Benny for sending me there. Not one little bit.

"Can I get in the water, Johnny? Please? It's awful hot."

Nobody but Carlotta called John Plonsky "Johnny." He'd been making low-budget monster flicks since Dracula was a boy, and he'd earned the respect of everyone in Hollywood except a few brainless starlets like this one.

Carlotta reached down into the water. Gathering a few drops in her cupped hand, she tried to dribble them across her front. I was too quick for her. I grabbed her wrist just in time to keep her from spoiling the pristine white bathing suit sheathing her perfect form. Every one of those drops would show on camera. In the time it took them to dry, Carlotta would start to sweat, and sweat stains are obvious on film.

The whole crew would be drawing their salaries while I escorted Carlotta to the hotel for a new suit and while I stood outside her dressing room, urging her to hurry. If Benny had foreseen this problem, there'd have been a clause in her contract requiring her to let me into the dressing room. I'm sure I could have poured her ample form into yet another tiny suit in a time-efficient manner.

Fortunately, I had brought way more bathing suits than I should have needed for this gig. (I'd worked with Carlotta before.) Otherwise, I'd have spent my days handwashing little scraps of white fabric, then waving them frantically in the muggy air till they dried.

She'd pulled this stunt once that day, already. John needed to shoot the sequence before she messed herself up again, and everybody knew it. I could see it on their faces as I hovered within arm's-reach, ready to stop her before she splashed river water on herself yet again.

We were all as hot as Carlotta. Hotter, actually, be cause we were wearing more clothes. If I let her mess up another bathing suit...well, one of these people just might shoot her.

"She can't work under these conditions, John," Carlotta's manager Bradley barked, adjusting his Panama hat to shade his face better. Her boyfriend Vince, who was bankrolling the film, adjusted his own Panama hat, which was bigger, more finely woven, and obviously more expensive.

John gestured at his uncooperative star, but spoke to the men in her life. "I just need her to sit still long enough for Louise to snatch her off the boat. Then she can go fan herself in her dressing room. Debbie can do the rest of the scene."

Louise and Debbie sat on the dock, chatting pleasantly about whatever it is that interests twenty-year-old girls. They were as blonde as Carlotta (whose real name was probably as plain as "Louise" or "Debbie") and they were as shapely. Debbie, in particular, looked just like her. This was her job.

When Debbie was struggling underwater in the monster's clutches, wet and half-dressed, moviegoers needed to believe they were watching Carlotta in mortal distress. Fortunately, Debbie was a very good actress. She could make you believe just about anything. In fact, she'd spent the last three weeks making me believe she was in love with me.

Louise, on the other hand, didn't look like Carlotta, nor any other woman of my acquaintance. She was heavily muscled and six feet tall, but perfectly proportioned for her size. The other two girls made men want to hug them and squeeze them and stroke them and romance them. Louise made you want to worship her for the goddess that she was.

And what was Louise's job on this movie set?

She was the monster.

When I told Benny that the monster needed no makeup artist, because the actor inside its rubber suit was completely invisible, I wasn't lying. Louise was a local girl who'd learned to swim in this fast-moving river. She could plunge to the bottom of the mammoth spring, swimming against the rushing water with powerful kicks and strokes. And she looked like a river nymph all the while, with her golden hair streaming behind her and her golden-skinned body slipping through the water like a shimmering fish.

Louise was a hundred percent suited to be the monster star of this movie, and she worked cheap. The crew for this movie was a hundred percent male, except for Carlotta and Debbie, and we approved John's decision to hire Louise a hundred percent. Actually, we thought he was a goddamn genius.

Lester Bond, owner of Glitter Spring and of the lodge perched on its rim, was a frustrated man. He'd bought the property with visions of a tourist attraction like Silver Springs. Hordes of paying customers, a fleet of glass-bottomed boats, hamburger stands, gator wrestling shows —if there was a Florida-tested method of separating Northerners from their money, Lester had hoped to build it on the shores of Glitter Spring.

Unfortunately, Lester wasn't a genius. He'd neglected to check the highway system funneling tourists into Florida's peninsula. Glitter Spring was just too far from a major tourist route, too far from an airport, too far from a decent-sized town. It was just too far from everything. When God made this jaw-dropping miracle of nature, He wasn't thinking like a grasping, avaricious human being, so He'd failed to put His miracle in a convenient spot. Lester Bond had stopped going to church, because he was really angry at the Almighty about this oversight.

Because of its inconvenient location, Glitter Spring sat out in the woods looking beautiful, all by its lonesome, like an old maid in a small town where all the good men were taken. If the spring's crystalline waters hadn't been tailor-made for underwater filming, Lester would have been bankrupt long before I met him. Only the likes of Tarzan and Esther Williams had brought in enough money to keep Lester's dream alive.

Evenings in the lobby of Lester's hotel weren't anything to write home about, especially when your home was Tinseltown. After dinner, we'd watch the dailies, and then Lester would turn up the lights. Air conditioning was a distant dream in 1940s Florida, so the lobby was gaspingly hot, even after dark. Still, we were young and we couldn't conceive of going to bed early, so we cranked up the electric fans and played cards or charades or board games. Sometimes, we just drank.

Lester played piano. It would have been nice if someone had sung, but Carlotta wasn't the kind of star with talents beyond looking good on camera. And she wasn't the kind of star who tolerated anyone else in the limelight. So if Louise or Debbie or anyone else possessed any hidden musical talent, they never showed it.

On that last peaceful evening, we were playing cards. Bridge tables were scattered around the lobby, and we'd been playing long enough that everybody'd had a turn at being dummy...which meant that everybody had spent time away from the other players' watchful eyes. Those who preferred drinking to cardplaying had wandered constantly to the bar and back, making their movements even more impossible to track. I believe that Carlotta and Louise went missing while the dailies were being screened, but there's no way to know for sure.

It says something about my devotion to the game of bridge that I had to look around for my girlfriend when I learned that Carlotta was gone. Or maybe it says something about my devotion to my girlfriend. But our three weeks of passion had left me under the *impression* that I loved Debbie.

Anyway, Debbie was across the room chatting with John about how she could act *and* do stunts, in case he needed somebody like that for his next picture. It's fortunate for me that Debbie didn't disappear that evening, or I'd have been left with the guilt and embarrassment of knowing my girlfriend went missing right under my own nose. Vince wasn't so lucky.

I'll give Vince credit for being a better boyfriend than me. He'd been passed out on the sofa for hours, but he'd gone looking for his lady love immediately upon regaining consciousness. When he couldn't find Carlotta in the hotel, he knew something was wrong. That city-bred woman would never have ventured out into the swamp alone.

Louise hadn't yet found a boyfriend among the crew, astonishing as it may sound. The sheer size of her scared the heck out of most guys. I myself was taller than Louise by a good three inches, but she still scared me now and again. We'd been looking for Carlotta for an hour before anybody noticed that Louise was gone, too. I wasn't sure how worried to be about big, strong, competent Louise, until I remembered the size of the alligators living on the far side of Glitter Spring. They could have swallowed that strapping girl alive.

"What could have happened?" Vince asked, his voice tinged by the kind of visceral, physical fear that didn't often bother people in Hollywood. "They were here and now they're just...not."

Everyone's eyes strayed to the black, leathery body of Ol' Jack, the enormous one-eyed alligator that Lester had paid somebody to shoot and stuff and mount. Ol' Jack dominated the spacious lobby, and his glass eyes glittered as if he knew how good humans tasted. In an instant, we ceased to be a convivial crowd of cardplaying drunks. In that instant, we began to be afraid.

When sudden death reaches out its monster hand, confusion descends. On that moonless night, both darkness and confusion were utterly complete.

As I've said, Lester's resort was a million miles from nowhere, which explained its stunning commercial success. This meant there was no light beyond the bright windows of the hotel and the glittering stars overhead.

Lester was accustomed to this kind of darkness. We Hollywood folk were not. He flung open his utility closet and handed out lanterns and flashlights. The swamp was alight as we crisscrossed the countryside, calling out for Carlotta and Louise. If there was any clue to their whereabouts, it was invisible in the dark and we trampled it.

At every turn, my lantern reflected off the glowing green eyes of alligators lurking under palmettos or floating in still waters. The light seemed to keep them at bay. I wondered if Carlotta had brought a lantern with her. I would never have ventured into that wilderness without one, not even on the promise of a screenwriting contract.

Eventually, we found Louise. I found her, actually. She was perched high in a deerhunting stand, clutching a burned-out flashlight. She was weeping and she wouldn't tell me why, but that magnificent Amazon body was unharmed.

Amazon or not, Louise was heartsore. I escorted her along the riverbank, with a gentlemanly arm around her waist. This did not endear me to Debbie. When she saw us coming, she slipped a ladylike hand into the crook of my other arm and clamped down hard on the soft flesh of my inner elbow. The two of us escorted Louise the rest of the way back.

Everyone was relieved to see Louise safe, but she was the only beautiful woman found in the swamps around Glitter Spring that evening. We all lay awake that night, wondering what had become of the biggest movie star for miles around.

At sunrise, Carlotta was still missing. The sheriff and his deputies were puttering around as if they knew what they were doing. John, on the other hand, was stumped.

"Do I keep filming? Or do I shut the movie down and send people home?" he asked me.

He'd asked those questions all night long, seeking guidance from the bigwigs in Hollywood. He got helpful answers like, "*No!!!* Don't keep filming! You can't keep spending money on a film that's lost its star," and "Of course, you gotta keep filming!! Do you know how much it's *costing* us to keep that crew in Florida??"

John was an artist, even on a low budget. He'd had all night to develop a plan. "I've gotta presume Carlotta's out in the swamp pouting and she'll be back any minute, ready for her close-up. But if I'm wrong, I think I can save the movie. We shot the last of her close-ups yesterday. Debbie was going to do most of the remaining scenes, anyway. I might have to finesse a few shots...you know...put a hat on Debbie or shoot her from behind, but it should work."

"Debbie's gonna want a raise," I said, because I was her boyfriend and I felt like I should look out for her.

"She's already asked for it. Got it, too," said John.

It seemed that Debbie didn't need her boyfriend all that much. Fortunately, I've always liked self-sufficient women.

At John's instruction, we boarded the boat that took us out to the calm lagoon where much of the movie had already been filmed. The empty monster suit lay on the deck where I always left it. I'd hauled it back and forth to the hotel for the first couple of nights, until I'd had a chance to stop and think. Who, in the middle of the Florida swamp, was going to take it? And what could possibly hurt the thing? It was made of rubber.

We were silent and businesslike. We could probably have made the movie even more cheaply if we'd always been so focused on the movie. It felt far better to work than to wonder what had happened to Carlotta.

John planned to film some scenes with Louise in the monster suit, hauling a kicking-and-screaming Debbie deep into the lagoon. It was a good plan, until Louise started to get dressed. She was carefully unzipping the monster suit, ready to crawl in and be an actress, when she suddenly went off-script.

Flinging her arms over her face and screaming, it took Louise three long-legged strides to run the length of the boat and throw herself into the lagoon. There may have been alligators in that still water, but Louise was always more comfortable with nature's monsters than she was with the human kind.

The rest of us hovered around the half-open monster suit. We all knew what was in there, but I was the wardrobe guy. This put me in charge of the suit, so I was the one who had to finish unzipping the thing.

The fully open zipper exposed Carlotta's bare back. A couple of bruises marred her creamy white flesh, but they were nothing compared to the wound on her head. Her glorious blonde curls, matted with blood and muddy sand, spilled out of the opening.

The cameraman had been a seasoned newspaper photographer long before he got into pictures. Without even pausing to think, he swung the movie camera around and pointed it at Carlotta's body and the crowd hovering over it.

Nobody said anything. Since I was closest to the corpse, I felt some responsibility to respond to the ugliness at my feet. I had nothing to say except, "Somebody find the sheriff."

John, being a director, knew exactly what to say and do. He made eye contact with the cameraman and said simply, "Cut and wrap."

Later in my career, I worked on the set of *The Andy Griffith Show*. If only Andy had been the sheriff who investigated Carlotta's murder...

We could have used his homestyle, Southern-bred wisdom. Instead, we got a tobacco-chewing, Yankee-hating heap of ignorance named Sheriff Meany. (Really. That was his name.) He paced importantly across the hotel lobby, exuding all the warmth and charm of Ol' Jack the stuffed alligator. We suspects loitered, waiting to be questioned. I saw in seconds that Sheriff Meany would not be solving Carlotta's murder and that he was fully capable of arresting someone...anyone...just to get this job over and done with.

Since I had ambitions of someday scripting a courtroom drama, I felt compelled to solve this crime myself. I also object strenuously to the prosecution of innocent people, particular when I'm one of the innocents under scrutiny. So I took a clear-eyed look at the facts.

Carlotta's murderer was almost certainly a part of the movie crew or the hotel staff. Someone would have heard a car or boat motor if an outsider had slipped in. It was possible that someone had come in on foot or rowed upstream for miles against the significant current of the Glitter River, but my money said the killer had been in the hotel that evening.

That presumption still left several dozen possibilities, but few of those had anything to gain from Carlotta's death. Quite a few had something to lose. I decided that my investigation would revolve around people who were personally affected by Carlotta. They could be affected for good or ill, but my deciding question was this: Who *cared* about what happened to Carlotta? Because people rarely die at the hands of people who just don't care.

Her manager Bradley cared. Whether he cared about Carlotta herself was open to question. Perhaps he was distraught that his primary source of income was now dead and stuffed into a rubber monster suit. The witless sheriff had finally called a doctor to sedate the weeping man, who lay sprawled on a couch, one arm flung across his face.

I didn't like to admit it, but my girl Debbie cared. She'd bitterly resented Carlotta's conceited airs. I couldn't tell you how many times she'd told me, "I can do everything she does and more. I could carry this picture. And I'm a professional. You wouldn't catch me whining about the heat or forgetting my lines. I just need a chance to show John what I can do."

Well, now Debbie had her chance. Fortunately, she was too dainty to stuff a hundred-and-twenty pounds of dead weight into a monster suit...but Louise wasn't. And Louise was huddled in a chair with her head under a blanket, trying to hide the fact that she hadn't stopped weeping since she was found alone in the swamp.

That distress was probably going to send Louise to jail by lunchtime, because Sheriff Meany seemed to see her tears as proof of guilt. And Louise's refusal to say why she'd been alone in a deer stand at midnight wasn't helping.

I myself had my eye on Vince, Carlotta's so-called boyfriend. Displaying the reptilian heart of your average Hollywood citizen, he'd spent the morning on the phone, checking to see whether the movie was insured for the murder of its star. Once his insurance coverage was confirmed, he looked relaxed and almost happy.

John, to his credit, had shed his own reptilian armor the instant Carlotta's body was found. While there was a reasonable chance she was alive, he'd continued his businesslike efforts to get his movie made and to get it made within budget. Once she was unquestionably dead, he'd reverted to being a human being.

There had been a tenderness in his tolerance for Carlotta's silliness that made me believe he cared for her. I was also convinced by the pain in his eyes. Don't forget that I made my living designing faces. I read them better than most people.

John glanced in my direction and I shifted my eyes away. Bradley fell into my field of vision, which worked well for me. Unconscious on the couch, he was hardly likely to yell at me for staring at him.

Bradley shifted in his sleep and his arm fell away from his face. The makeup artist in me was so startled that I quit sneaking glances and frankly stared. The whole right side of his face was pink and puffy. Yeah, he'd had his arm resting on his face for awhile, but not *that* long. And his arm would not have made the five separate welts extending from his cheek to his hairline.

I spent a lot of my days repairing famous faces that had gotten themselves slapped. I recognized the pattern on Bradley's face. Trust me.

Men don't ordinarily go around slapping other men, and I knew only one woman for miles around capable of inflicting that kind of damage with one strike. I was pretty sure I knew who had made Louise cry. The question was why.

I was relieved to see that Louise had quit weeping. Tears aren't any more tragic on a pretty face than on a homely one, but I'm a man, after all. I would have wrestled a gator for Louise's entertainment, just to keep the tears off that lovely face.

Sheriff Meany was not pleased to see me escort his prime suspect out of the lobby, but he let us leave. The man had deputies guarding the exits, the parking lot, and the dock. Louise and I weren't going anywhere.

Ignoring 1940s propriety, I hustled Louise into her room and closed the door.

I patted her on the hand, then got straight to the point. "I know who you were with last night, and I don't think you killed Carlotta. I just have one question: Why did you slap Bradley silly?"

She looked at the palm of her hand as if it still stung. "Why do women usually slap men?"

"Because they get fresh?"

She laughed. "Oh, Bradley's been trying to get fresh for weeks. I kinda like it, or I never would've agreed to meet him last night. No, I slapped him because of the lipstick on his collar. Some woman wiped her face on Bradley so well that I could see the smear in the dark, with just my flashlight."

Lipstick? I was a makeup artist. Now the woman was talking my language.

"What color lipstick? I guess it wasn't your color, or you wouldn't have slapped him."

"Brownish-red," she said in a mildly revolted tone of voice. I understood her revulsion. That color would have been ghastly against her blonde hair and golden complexion...which meant that it didn't belong to Louise or Carlotta, either. If I'd smeared that color on the lips of any of the three blonde sirens making this movie, John would have confiscated my makeup bag and sent me back to Hollywood.

Was Bradley's lover on the hotel staff? Hardly. The cook was on the wrong side of seventy. I'd wager that the austere housekeeper's pale skin had never made the acquaintance of any cosmetic beyond bar soap. And both waitresses were dark-skinned brunettes who favored cherry-red lips, because cheap, loud makeup attracts big-tipping men. Very few women could get away with lipstick the color of dried blood.

Dried blood...

What had Louise really seen on Bradley's collar?

Sheriff Meany didn't like Bradley's looks, so it wasn't hard to convince him to ask the man to produce his shirt. Bradley had progressed quickly from his first response, "I can't find it," to his final response, "You'll have to talk to my lawyer about that."

Sheriff Meany wasn't completely stupid. He knew that a man who was unable to find a just-worn shirt in a small hotel room was a man who was hiding something. Looking at me with an expression approaching respect, he asked, "You got any more bright ideas?"

"Have you found the murder weapon?"

"From the looks of the wound and the mud around it, I'm thinking the killer used a rock. Unless he was an idiot, he killed her with it, then dropped it in the river. The whole river bed's limestone. The murder weapon won't look any different from any other rock, not after the river's washed the blood off."

"Could you look for the spot where the killer *got* the rock?"

The sheriff opened his mouth to call me an idiot, then closed it. Because if you thought about it, there were only a few places that made any sense at all. There were some good-sized rocks used for landscaping around the hotel grounds, and there were plenty of rocks along the riverside. That was about it. Why would anybody walk into the vermin-infested swamp and away from the river and its perfectly good rocks?

It didn't take long for Meany's deputies to find a damp hole in the riverbank. The muddy sand at the bottom was the same pale color as the mud on poor Carlotta's head. I was feeling very proud of my deductive prowess, until Meany mentioned another clue that I quite frankly never saw coming.

Love is indeed blind, because it never occurred to me that the footprint in the muddy sand next to that damp hole would be dainty and feminine. It just never crossed my mind that this print would perfectly match my sweet Debbie's shapely foot.

When you spoon-fed Sheriff Meany a seamless sequence of clues, then led him patiently to their correct solution, he could be made to see the truth. Debbie and Bradley had been carrying on the kind of affair often seen in Hollywood. He was losing his hold on the client who served as his gravy train. She was pretty and ambitious as hell. Together, they'd planned to seize Hollywood's attention and keep it.

With Carlotta dead, Vince's insurers would have made certain the picture got made. By killing Carlotta as soon as her closeups were filmed, Debbie was set to walk right into the starring role for the remainder of filming. John already liked her work. The odds were good that he'd start to see her as leading lady material, and a star would be born. Or so Debbie and her ambitious new manager hoped.

Bradley had been sleeping with Carlotta for years. It had been his price for taking her as a client in the first place. During our weeks in Florida, he'd taken Debbie on as a new client...and extracted the same price. The two of them must have been blessed with rare vigor, since their trysts had taken place after he left Carlotta's bed and she left mine.

At first, I thought that Bradley had been trying to add Louise to his stable of client/lovers. Taking on a woman as physically daunting as Louise on a night when he'd already visited Carlotta and Debbie would have been...impressive...so I was crediting Bradley with stupendous vigor until I saw the subtlety of what he'd done.

He'd seduced Louise and taken her into the swamp by boat for their rendezvous. Carlotta was already dead by this time, because her blood on his collar had gotten him slapped. This fight with Louise had made it that much easier to do what he'd always intended...leave her in the deer stand with a burned-out flashlight and no safe way to get back to the hotel. No Florida girl would go wading alone through gator territory in the dark. When she was eventually found, not far from the murder site, she'd be an obvious suspect for Carlotta's murder. She'd have been presumed to be as murderously jealous of Carlotta as Debbie was, and she was a lot more physically capable of murder.

And how did the two conspirators actually commit the crime? The sheriff eventually found a faint smear of blood proving that the murder happened on the boat. I presume that Bradley used his stupendously vigorous charms to lure Carlotta into a passionate embrace and that Debbie sneaked up behind her and whammed a muddy rock onto her head. A bit of blood must have gotten onto Bradley's collar, and probably a whole lot of gore got onto Debbie. We found one of the little teeny bathing suits I bought her, bloodstained and wrapped in Bradley's shirt, buried under a cypress tree downstream from the hotel.

When faced with that bundle of clothing, Bradley told us everything, hoping for mercy since he didn't do the actual killing. Debbie never said a word.

She didn't need to speak. I knew the truth when I saw the dailies.

It was not a good day for shooting a picture. We only got thirty seconds of film...but that half-minute tells a hell of a story. It begins with a blur as the quick-witted cameraman whipped around and caught the wordless horror on Louise's face as she ran from the monster suit and its hideous contents. Proving that he was an artist with a lens, he pulled back just a bit and focused on our faces as the rest of us took a long dark look into the abyss.

I can still see the scene he captured. It is etched on my retinas, my mind, my heart. This moment, which will never shine down at an audience from a silver screen, is the moment when our low-budget monster flick reached the level of true art.

John's face is a study in heartbreak.

Vince stares down at the bloody nothingness that had been his lover. He communicates no feeling. He just looks like he wants to be sick.

Debbie and Bradley aren't looking at Carlotta at all, because they've already seen the monstrosity hiding in that pitiful rubber suit. They're looking into each other's faces. I've looked at that still shot a million times, and I still can't tell whether their eyes are communicating love or fear or loathing. I've come to think that murderers aren't capable of love or fear, not really. Every emotion for them is some form of loathing.

And where did my gaze turn in that stomach-churning instant? My eyes aren't focused on Carlotta or her killers. They're not focused on anything in range of the camera. I'm looking past the cameraman, down the boat's long deck where Louise just fled from the sight of death. I'm looking for the only woman I have ever loved.

I did get my dream career as a screenwriter, though I can't say it was completely on my own merits. It never hurts to be the spouse of a bankable star. Though Louise never displaced Esther Williams as queen of the movie mermaids, she was always bankable. And she was always lovable. When she turned those wide blue eyes on the camera, her sweet nature showed through, and movie audiences loved her almost as much as I did.

Her acting coaches drummed the rural Florida accent out of her, but she can still turn it back on for me. She knows how much I like to hear her say, "Ah love yew, darlin'."

And I answer her, in my flat Tinseltown tones, saying, "I love you too, darling. And I always have...ever since I first saw you wearing that stupid rubber monster suit."

When Michael Lister approached me about doing a story for Florida Heat Wave, *I was pleased, both because I like working with Michael and because, as I've said, I like writing short stories. I had a single, teeny, tiny concern for this project, though. I'd already written a story set in Florida for Michael—"Mouse House," which is set in Orlando. That story had to be set in Florida, since it was for an anthology called* North Florida Noir. *I had no choice in the matter.*

I'd also written "A Singularly Unsuitable Word" for an anthology called A Kudzu Christmas *and, although it didn't absolutely have to be set in Florida, the "kudzu" in the title tells you that this story had, by God, better be set in the South. And the title also indicates that it better, by God, be set at Christmastime. The story needed a setting that would be warm and steamy at Christmastime, so I'd chosen a Florida backdrop for that story, as well.*

And, for A Merry Band of Murderers, *I'd also written the first story in this collection: "Land of the Flowers." "Land of the Flowers" isn't just set in Florida. As its title suggests, it's about Florida. In fact, it's my love letter to my adopted state, a place that's damn close to being cherished to death.*

So now Michael wanted me to write another story set in Florida, and I wasn't altogether sure I had anything left to say about the place, particularly in light of the fact that I had also, at that time, already written a couple of novels set here. And I was researching a third.

This, I thought, could be a problem.

Fortunately, my book research for Strangers took me in an unexpected direction. I learned that St. Augustine had been a center of moviemaking during the silent movie days. Portions of The Perils of Pauline *had been filmed there. Theda Bara and Rudolph Valentino acted there. I could definitely see fodder for a story buried in all that information, but I was reluctant to cannibalize the research I was doing for* Strangers. *(And I was right. I did use St. Augustine's movie history in* Strangers, *so it would have been a mistake to use it in this story, too.)*

But the artistic process is a funny thing. Once I got started thinking about movies, I remembered so many other movies filmed here in the Sunshine State, and one of them was The Creature from the Black Lagoon. *This seemed perfect for a noir anthology, since a 1940s horror flick calls to mind a time that itself seems noir, simply because our memories of it were recorded in black-and-white.*

I began thinking of a story set in a place very like Wakulla Springs, during the filming of a movie very like The Creature from the Black Lagoon. *When I imagined a character who was charged with taking care of the monster suit and when I realized that the suit was a perfectly noir place to hide a body, I knew I had my story.*

Something tells me that I'll never run out of things to say about Florida

– Mary Anna

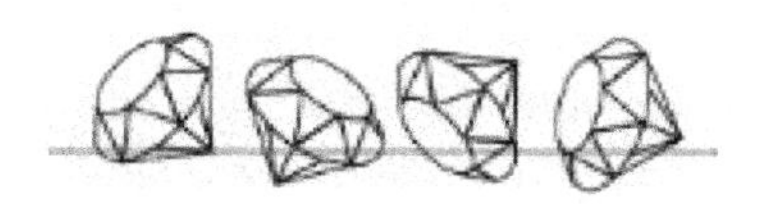

STEALING MONA

You may have noticed that I titled this book Jewel Box: Short Works by Mary Anna Evans, *when I could just have well given it the title* Jewel Box: Short Fiction by Mary Anna Evans. *I'm a novelist. Wouldn't my short works be fiction by definition?*

Not necessarily.

Occasionally, novelists are invited to write essays. Mystery novelists tend to be invited to write essays about mystery fiction, essays that address the question of what mystery fiction is. How does it work? Why is it so much fun to read? Being a scholarly sort, I thrive on questions like these.

The following essay was written for an issue of Mystery Readers Journal *that was dedicated to the relationship between mysteries and art.* Mystery Readers Journal *specializes in asking and answering such esoteric and interesting subjects. In "Stealing Mona," I use art as a catalyst for a subject to which I have returned more than once: Can a mystery without a murder work?*

There are many crimes in this world, and not all of them are murder. Does somebody really have to die for a piece of crime fiction to be successful? This essay is one answer to that question. Believe me, I have others...

– Mary Anna

STEALING MONA

Crime fiction is, for good or ill, inextricably linked to a single crime: murder. Murder is momentous and irreversible. Nothing engages the attention of a human being more than the threat of death. Other crimes pale in comparison.

If I asked you to name a crime other than murder that could support an entire novel, the list would be short—so short, in fact, that I'll bet I can predict one of the first candidate crimes to cross your mind: the theft of the Mona Lisa. Yes, she's been stolen before in books, in movies, and in real life, and I daresay there are stories on the subject yet to be told. But why?

Because Mona is irreplaceable. The French government doesn't even hold an insurance policy on her, because she is literally priceless. Stealing her would be a crime against humanity, a special-interest group that presumably includes anyone reading this book. I think most of us agree that murder is still a more significant crime, but stealing the Mona Lisa (or nuking the Taj Mahal or burning a Gutenberg Bible) would certainly grab a reader's attention.

And that is why I would argue for a special connection between mystery fiction and the art world. Like a human life, a work of art is inherently irreplaceable.

Which scene would you read with more interest—the highjacking of an armored truck carrying many millions of dollars, or the highjacking of an armored truck carrying

Michelangelo's statue of David? (Yes, I know it would have to be a big, honking armored truck, but humor me.)

It would be a great hardship for somebody to lose all that money but, in the end, it's only money. The chunk of marble that is this particular statue of David connects us with everyone else who ever admired its beauty. What is more, the statue connects us with Michelangelo Buonarotti, the man. (Did you know that the restorers of the Sistine Chapel ceiling found bristles from his brush embedded in the frescoes he painted nearly 500 years ago? Or that they found the indentations made by his fingers as he felt the fresh plaster, checking to see whether it was ready for painting? Michelangelo's actual fingerprints, made by his actual fingers...is that cool or what?)

Art is about human connections.

Dashiell Hammett's *The Maltese Falcon*, one of the mystery field's most classic works, exploits the fact that a work of art is so much more than its component parts. Yes, the Falcon was encrusted with jewels, but its great age and its romantic association with the Knights Templar of Malta took a pretty bauble and made it priceless. A contemporary work, Joanne Dobson's *The Maltese Manuscript*, turned this idea on its head. In Dobson's book, an original manuscript of *The Maltese Falcon*, annotated by Hammett's own hand, is catapulted from a stack of ink-stained paper into an irreplaceable work of art for which people will kill.

While researching my second novel, *Relics*, I found myself hip-deep in information on art forgery. (Why? I can't tell you.)

Successful art forgery requires talent and time that could have been used to create original art. Since original art is, unfortunately, worth nearly nothing when the artist is unknown, turning to forgery is understandable if you're the talented but dishonest sort. But why forge a Picasso or a Monet? Why not use that artistic talent to create, say, a stack of perfect portraits of Benjamin Franklin? Why not just forge money?

Ignoring the technical difficulties of producing counterfeit cash, I'll venture this as an answer: because money has a finite value and great art is without price.

Having made that point, I'll close by telling you that *Relics,* my own foray into the labyrinthine world of art forgery, required me to learn a prodigious amount about the production of tin-glazed lusterware ceramic art in the medieval Islamic world.

Don't ask me why. If I told you, I'd have to kill you. Or steal your most prized work of art...

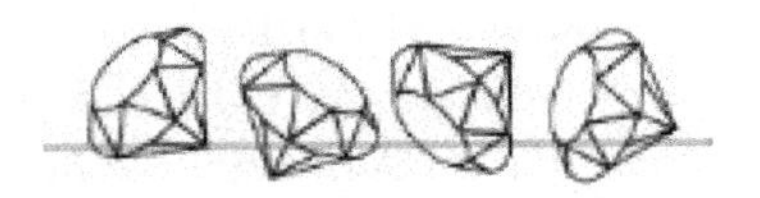

A SINGULARLY UNSUITABLE WORD

The first short story I wrote as an adult was written from the point-of-view of an elderly man remembering events from his youth. I find myself returning to this style, time and again. There are three very different stories in this volume that are told as reminiscences—"Low-Budget Monster Flick," "Starch" and "A Singularly Unsuitable Word," and I frequently have historical passages related by elderly people in my novels that could stand alone as short stories. I've included one of those tales later in this book, an excerpt from Artifacts *called "Cally's Story," just to see for myself whether it really could work as a story on its own. I think it does.*

I recently read a wonderful book called Water for Elephants *that was a well-deserved bestseller. Imagine my pleasure to see that Sarah Gruen enjoyed that same technique well enough to write her book in that style*

Lila, the viewpoint character in "A Singularly Unsuitable Word" wants to tell you about a time that is within living memory, yet is so different as to seem like an alien world. In this world, there are no televisions or radios impinging on parents' ability to protect their children's innocence. It is a world in which no one can conceive that a child from a good family might have ever heard language that belongs in a gutter. And it is a world where one of those singularly unsuitable words has the power to save an innocent young man's life.

– Mary Anna

A SINGULARLY UNSUITABLE WORD

I am so old that I remember when ladies didn't swear or drive automobiles. I recall a time when a young lady was considered fast if she let a boy hold her hand before he slid an engagement ring onto it. I'll be blunt. I remember Prohibition. How old do you reckon that makes me?

I remember my childhood, too, in a blurry kind of way. There were no hard edges in those days for little girls who were lucky, like me. There was no television to bring the world into my home, so I thought everybody had chickens and cows and vegetable gardens that gave them all they needed to eat. I saw no reason why all children wouldn't have two or three toys to play with, just like I did. I was Florida-bred so, though I could well imagine that other folks might sweat occasionally—I certainly did—I had no notion of what it might mean to be cold.

I went to Sunday School weekly, so I knew that there were bad things that I shouldn't do. Still, for the first eight years of my life, those bad things were just numbers on the commandment list. What did killing and stealing and taking the Lord's name in vain have to do with me?

Perhaps my eight-year-old self was aware that I was infringing on one of those commandments when I filched a cookie shaped like a candy cane and crept out into that warm December night. Even now, I'm not sure which commandment covers spying on your sister, but one of them must. I knew that I shouldn't be creeping around in my nightgown, following Iris as she crept down the river path wearing hers. I justified my actions by telling God (and Santa Claus, whose sleigh was probably on its way to my house right that minute) that if seventeen-year-old Iris couldn't manage to stay in the house when she was supposed to be asleep, then how could I?

I tried to be quiet as I skulked down the damp trail, but Florida riverbank foliage is lush and overgrown, even in wintertime. Iris should have been able to hear the spider lilies and palmettos rustle like crinolines as I pushed past them, but her mind was on something else. When she reached the landing, I saw what that something else was. Except it wasn't a "something" else. It was a "someone" else.

He was older than Iris. I would have called him a man, and Iris was, in my eyes, just a girl. And a silly one at that. He wore a driving cap pulled low over his eyes, and a glen plaid vest that was so fashionable that it must have come from a city. Maybe Tallahassee. Pensacola, even.

I was glad to see that he was gentleman enough to take off his cap when he saw Iris coming. Then he tossed that fancy cap into the bottom of his flat-bottomed boat, stepped onto the landing, wrapped his arms around Iris, and commenced doing some ungentlemanly things. After a time, his behavior turned quite ungentlemanly—I'll refrain from discussing her behavior completely, if you don't mind —and there I sat, stuck in the palmettos until they got finished with whatever it was they were doing.

When the other boat arrived, they were in no condition to hear it coming, particularly since the two men piloting it came from upstream with their motor off, poling it silently into place beside the dock. With a careless motion, the thin, dark-haired man standing in front tied the heavily loaded boat to a handy cleat.

"And here I thought your deliveries was slow 'cause you was cheating me," said the burly man standing in back with his hand on the rudder. "Shit, Owen. You was just passing the time with this young slut."

The young man lunged toward him with both fists balled up, but he never got to use them. Fists aren't a whole lot of good against a revolver.

Owen, who suddenly looked less like a man and more like a boy, went dead still when the burly man pulled his gun. I swear, he stopped moving so fast that he was left standing on one foot, with the other hanging in the air behind him. Iris, who had been busily arranging her nightgown, which was in quite some disarray, started screaming. The sound stirred the hairs on the back of my neck.

"Come to think of it," the gunman said, "maybe I want to spend some time with the slut, too." His hand shot out and grabbed Iris by the waist. He showed that he'd spent a lifetime on the water by hauling her into the boat, one-handed, without flipping the blamed thing. Also, it was a mighty big boat.

"Leave the girl alone, Gibson," his partner whined. "This'll get us nothing but trouble."

"Shut up," Gibson said, and I was relieved to see the gun swing away from Owen toward this man I didn't know. This makes no sense, since I didn't know Owen, either, but Iris did (quite well, it appeared) and that made him almost kin.

"I'm done with the two of you," Gibson said, waving the revolver back and forth between Owen and the other man, whom I suddenly recognized. It was Mr. Robbins, who worked at the sawmill in town. "You're cheating me, the both of you."

"How can you say that?" Mr. Robbins asked. His eyes bugged out of his long sallow face every time the gun swung his way. "I go over the numbers with you every night. We count the bottles together before we deliver them. We count the money together when we get home. Then we pay Owen and we split the rest. How could we cheat you?"

Gibson's eyes flicked away toward the woods for a second, and I recognized two things in those eyes that scared me. First, they were unfocused, the way my grandfather's got when he'd had too much rum. And second, they showed a peculiar mix of confusion and humiliation that I'd seen before.

My friend Jeremy, Daddy's fieldhand, had come home one day with that self-same look on his face. It was the day he got tricked into paying a dime for a little old candy bar because he didn't know his numbers. After that, I made it my business to walk to the store with him and look over the clerk's shoulder while he totted up Jeremy's receipt. Eight-year-old girls can get away with most anything when they smile, and everybody in town knew I'd been able to add a double-column of numbers since I was six.

I'd been real proud of my tidy solution to Jeremy's problem, but on that night I felt as cold and rudderless as if I'd been dumped into the muddy river below me. I wrapped my arms around my knees and tried not to shiver. If my shaking set the spider lilies and palmettos to moving, then Gibson would know I was there. I didn't intend for him to be pointing that gun at me, too.

He was going to shoot them—Owen and Mr. Robbins, and maybe Iris, too. That shamed, angry light in his eyes said that he saw no other choice. He needed the other men to help him run his business because he couldn't count the money, but he couldn't trust them not to cheat him... because he couldn't count the money.

Owen had finally eased his airborne foot down onto the landing, but his stance was odd and stiff, just like you'd expect of a man being held at gunpoint. Still, there was something funny about his right arm. He was holding it about a foot in front of him, with the palm pointed in toward his belly. Since I was situated where I could see that belly in profile, I was well-positioned to see something that Gibson couldn't—a bulge beneath that glen plaid vest. If Gibson was distracted, just for a moment, Owen might be able to save my sister, and himself, too.

I needed something to throw. A shoe would be perfect, but I wasn't wearing anything but my nightgown and underdrawers. I would have thrown them and sat there stark naked, except I couldn't imagine that they would make much noise.

Being as how Florida is nothing but a spit of sand, there were no handy rocks, but our swamps are full of cypress balls. I hefted one of them, a hard green knob about the size of a baseball, and heaved it into the river. It landed near Mr. Robbins' end of the boat, which turned out to be an altogether bad thing for him. Gibson hollered out a word I'd never heard before and pulled the trigger without a moment's thought, hitting Mr. Robbins square in the middle of his chest.

Poor Mr. Robbins toppled overboard and sank like a rock. Even though my sister was in the worst trouble imaginable and I wasn't in a much more secure position myself, there was a long heartbeat when all I could think about was Ginny Robbins, who was two grades ahead of me in school. She didn't deserve the news she was going to get come morning.

Now, let me tell you about the word Gibson said when he pulled the trigger, because it'll be important later on. In the years since then, I've heard that word several times. Not a lot, because people used to have some discretion about swearing in front of ladies. Certainly not lately, because you'd have to be some kind of a buffoon to swear in front of a doddering old woman like me. But now and then, someone has let it slip, so I've heard it and I know what it means, but I've only let it cross my lips once. I don't intend to do it again, so you'll have to figure it out for yourself. It rhymes with "Love your truck." And it is a major violation of the commandment about honoring your mother.

At the instant Mr. Robbins lost his life, Owen went for his gun, but he took just a whisper too long to pull it clear of his waistband. Gibson's revolver went off again. Owen's shot went wild, and he pitched off the landing into the river. I don't recollect whether Iris had been screaming all the while, but she was making plenty of noise by this time, for sure. Gibson smacked her a good one, started the boat's motor, slipped it from its mooring, and headed upstream with my sister. By the time they passed out of sight, I reckon I was making as much noise with my blubbering as Iris was with hers. It was only when I stopped to breathe that I heard the gurgling sound in the water.

It is a blessing that Owen was shot in the arm, because that left him two legs and one good arm to help me drag him out of the water. I was an unusually smart little girl, but I wasn't as big as a minute.

He probably needed to sit there for a while and remember how to breathe, but there was no time. Gibson was hauling Iris upstream, but he had to navigate around a big oxbow and I knew a path that cut straight across the bend.

I grabbed Owen by his good arm and hustled him to the spot where he had a fighting chance to save my sister. He was cooperative, which was good, because I was hardnosed enough to twist his bad arm until he saw the light. He moved well for a man whose blood was dripping out and splashing on the ground. I knew that situation probably couldn't go on much longer, but we didn't have far to go. The path dead-ended at the river and, praise Jesus, we had gotten there fast enough.

The bank we stood on rose five feet above the river. We could have leaned over and spit on Gibson, but I paused for a second to come up with a more constructive way to use this competitive advantage. Owen was ordinarily a very smart man but, as a thinker, this wasn't his finest hour. He didn't stop to plan; he just launched himself, feet-first, at a man holding a gun who had just proven himself capable of murder.

As I've said, the boat was fully loaded with cargo. The two men crashed so hard into one box that it busted open and let out a smell like the inside of my grandfather's flask. Even Gibson wasn't a good enough boatman to keep his vessel upright under this onslaught. Gibson, Owen, Iris—all three of them went into the river, and the fighting and cursing began in earnest.

I needed to help my sister, and I was going to need a distraction bigger than a cypress ball. I looked around for an idea and was rewarded. The riverbank sloped downward a few yards upstream until it was barely higher than the river itself, and the criminals in the boat below me had made good use of that fact. It was an ideal spot to unload boxes from a car directly into a boat, and the Model T Ford that they used to run their rum was still parked there, waiting for them. It was certainly bigger than a cypress ball, but I didn't have a clear idea how I could use it to save Iris and Owen. Yet.

As I ran for the car, I learned another curse word. It rhymes with "odd ma'am," and it is a serious transgression against the commandment against taking the Lord God's name in vain.

I must confess that the rescue plan I developed was at least as ill-considered as Owen's, but I was under duress. I was also eight years old.

It seemed to me that Owen and Iris were only a few feet from shore, and that perhaps I could just drive the car out there and get them. The car would provide me some protection from Gibson's gun, assuming the revolver was even still dry enough to shoot. Once Owen and Iris were in the car, we could flee at top speed—thirty miles an hour, maybe more. It did not occur to me to wonder whether an internal combustion engine would work any better underwater than a revolver would. Cars were, in those days, new and magical beasts.

Like most children, I watched and remembered each move the adults around me made, even when I didn't understand its purpose. I knew how to "advance the spark" so that the car would start. I knew that I would find the crank on the floorboard in front of the passenger seat. I knew how to fit it into the housing on the car's front and turn it. I knew that I would need to pull it away fast when the engine started, so as not to have my arm jerked off. However, I did not—and still do not—know much about the braking system of the Model T. At some point in the process, I disengaged the brake and, when I knelt in front of the car, crank in hand, it started to roll.

Iris, God bless her, was in the middle of the worst night of her life when she looked up and saw a car driving over her cherished baby sister. To this day, I can hear her screaming, "Lila! Lila, don't die—please don't die!" I have rarely felt so loved.

She might have known that I had sense enough to lay down real flat on the ground between the wheels and let the thing roll right over me.

A Model T splashing into a river makes a mighty fine distraction. Owen, who probably should have been more worried about me than he was, though perhaps he already knew me well enough to presume I'd be fine, took the opportunity to wrestle Gibson into a headlock.

The sound of a baying dog and a man's steady voice reached me, and I knew my daddy had heard the gunshot and had come to set things right. For all the years my father lived, I enjoyed the assurance that he would take care of Iris and me. That night was no different. Watched over by Daddy and also by his hunting rifle, his bird dog Sam, and Owen, Gibson was no trouble to any of us while we waited for the sheriff.

❖ ◆ ❖ ◆ ❖

Our ordeal should have been long past when the sheriff arrived. Quite a crowd had gathered on the river bank to gawk at Gibson by then—news travels fast in places where nothing interesting ever happens—and a more somber group had gathered downstream to look for Mr. Robbins. The sheriff listened soberly as Owen told his story, shaking his head at his description of how Gibson shot Mr. Robbins in cold blood.

Then Gibson raised his head and said, "The kid's lying. He shot Robbins, and then he tried to kill me. I shot him in self-defense."

I did not, at that time, fully realize the jeopardy that Owen was now in. In those days before fancy forensic work, I doubt that anyone in central Florida could have told whether the bullet that killed Mr. Robbins had come from Owen's gun or Gibson's. Assuming their guns could be fished up off the river bottom, I imagine the lawmen could have told that they'd both been fired, but that's about all. This case would be decided based on eyewitness testimony which, in my mind, wasn't going to be a problem. It wasn't a question of Owen's word against

Gibson's. Iris and I had both seen what happened. Once we got the chance to tell our stories, I knew that everyone would see the truth.

I didn't understand that Jeb Gibson was a man of substance and wealth in our county, and the fact that his wealth was built on rum running didn't bother people all that much. Truth be told, a lot of the gawking onlookers were his customers. Maybe the sheriff was, too, for all I know.

I also didn't understand that the word of an eight-year-old child meant nothing then. Still doesn't, actually. And the testimony of a seventeen-year-old girl who had been caught visiting with her boyfriend in her nightgown could hardly have been taken seriously, not in those days. Women had only been granted the right to vote and sit on juries during my sister's lifetime, so our word might have been suspect to that crowd, even if we'd been upstanding citizens of legal age. I didn't understand these matters, but I sensed that things weren't going Owen's way, so I leapt into the breach. This seems to have been my lifelong way of doing things.

"I saw him! I saw Gibson shoot Mr. Robbins, right in the chest."

Women started murmuring about how a child hadn't ought to see such awful sights. They were right, but that was water under the bridge now.

"Why would he do such a thing?" the sheriff asked, getting down on one knee beside me. I could tell by his tone of voice that he was just humoring me. He had no intention of letting a little girl interfere with the august processes of the law.

"He thought Mr. Robbins and Owen were cheating him. Mr. Robbins explained to him that they weren't and I believed him. I think—" I hesitated to expose Gibson's ignorance but he was a murderer and all, so I plunged ahead. "—I think he can't read and do his numbers, and he was afraid they were taking advantage."

I saw a couple of people, including the sheriff, flick their eyes at the ground, which told me that I wasn't the only one who knew Gibson's secret.

"Tell me exactly what happened," the sheriff said, so I did. I must have looked like an avenging cherub, standing there in a nightgown wet with riverwater and Owen's blood. I started at the beginning and I told the story.

Perhaps I went into too much detail regarding the things Owen and Iris were doing at the landing because, for a time, every eye was fastened on my sister's mortified face. But when I described the two men floating downriver on a boat loaded with contraband, those eyes swiveled in my direction. When I delivered—word for word—the argument between Gibson, Mr. Robbins, and Owen, people listened. When I got to the part where Gibson shot Mr. Robbins, his widow moaned. Still, I had the sense that I was failing. None of these people would decide which man to put in jail based on the word of a skinny girl-child.

I imbued my description of the shooting with every lurid detail I could recall. The red spray of blood from the victim's chest. The smell of gunpowder and mud. The lonely splash of a body striking water. They were there with me, watching the murder. I could see it in their eyes. Yet they could not muster the faith they needed to act. I was still not a plausible witness.

Then I dropped the final fact onto my teetering pile of details, and they believed. I told them what Gibson had said when he pulled the trigger.

Everyone there knew me. They knew my mama and my daddy. They could well believe that Iris was capable of misbehaving in the way I described, but they were equally certain that no eight-year-old girl from a good family could possibly know that loathsome word. Some of the women in the crowd turned uncertain eyes on their husbands because they, themselves, had never heard it.

Later, when I told my story to the judge, I had been advised of how singularly unsuitable that word was for a young lady. Or an old lady or a gentleman of any age, for that matter. I refused to say it again, but the sheriff had heard my testimony the first time, and he explained things to the judge for me.

Justice was served.

Owen did a little time for his rum running, but it was nothing compared to what he would have gotten for killing Mr. Robbins. I don't know if Gibson ever got out of prison. They may have hanged him, for all I know. This was not the kind of information that was shared with little girls in those long-ago times. Everyone concerned agreed that it was best to let Owen and Iris get married before he went off to jail. Just in case. She was waiting for him when he got home, and they lived together in a little house on the riverbank for the rest of their long lives.

Eventually, I stopped being a little girl and people started listening to me when I talked.

I take that back. After that night on the river, people paid heed to what I said, because I had proven myself. I believe some of them were a little afraid of me, which may have been why I came so near to being an old maid. Webster Simpson was the only man, other than my father, who could take me seriously without being afraid of me, so I married him. We lived next door to Iris and Owen for the rest of his long life, and we were happy.

Webster was a roofer by trade, but he was an artist at heart. There was nothing that man couldn't make with a piece of galvanized roofing and a pair of tin snips. He made Iris a toy Model T, complete with tires that rolled and a tiny little crank on the passenger floorboard. She hung it on her Christmas tree every year until she died.

It's hanging near the tip-top of my own Christmas tree, right this minute.

One of my trusted readers is a very intelligent and well-read man with a Ph.D. and many scholarly books to his credit. Nevertheless, he had a little trouble understanding Lila's ladylike way of telling you what those singularly unsuitable words were.

Really? I thought. A grown man can't figure out what she means when she refers to a cuss word by saying, "It rhymes with 'Love your truck.' And it is a major violation of the commandment about honoring your mother." And this one: "It rhymes with 'odd ma'am,' and it is a serious transgression against the commandment against taking the Lord God's name in vain."

Please don't ask me to believe that any of you seriously had any problem deciphering that. If you did, please go ask one of your children to serve as your interpreter, because I'm not telling you.

– Mary Anna

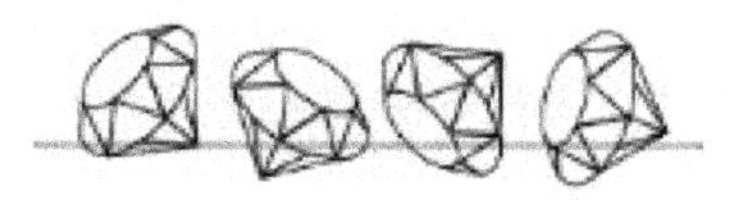

MOUSE HOUSE

As soon as I received the invitation to be part of the anthology North Florida Noir, *I was already thinking ahead, trying to decide what I was going to write. I wrote the editor, Michael Lister, and the rambling message said something like this: "Maybe I could set it at the beach? Or the swamp. The swamp is better, but everybody's gonna do the swamp..."*

Michael said, "You can stretch north Florida down to Orlando, if it would help," and that blessed light bulb went off in my head, the one that tells me I know exactly what story I want to tell.

I was going to kill somebody at...um...some nameless theme park that boasts a big tall castle. And somebody who really needed a comeuppance was going to get shoved off that big tall castle.

I could see that this was going to be fun....

– Mary Anna

MOUSE HOUSE

If Peter Pan had expired less flamboyantly or, better yet, if he had not expired at all, the murder of Paolo Arrezzo might have remained forever unsolved. If Peter Pan had stayed alive, it is possible (though unlikely) that Mr. Arrezzo's death certificate might always have read "cardiac arrest." Medical examiners tend to take special care with the post-mortem examinations of high-level Mafia officials who find themselves without a pulse at the tender age of 42, but there are many chemicals capable of rendering one dead. While the crime lab would certainly have looked for the poison that left him face-down in his apple strudel, some of them are damn hard to find unless you know precisely what noxious agent you're seeking.

Young Mr. Pan's cause of death was much easier to pinpoint. When a human being covered in fake fairy dust leaps out of a castle window, trusting that his safety cable will guide him gently to the ground, it's best for that cable to be in one piece. I was in my office, using a dozen security cameras to scan the excitable crowd below the unfortunate Pete, when the cable failed and sent him to his fate.

Parents snatched their children—some of them teenaged and quite large—and carried them bodily toward the park exit. Within ten seconds, Main Street was a bottleneck with the potential to kill hundreds of panic-stricken guests. In the array of security monitors, I could see my staff, efficient and well-trained, leap into action. Opening seldom-used gates, they began funneling guests down into the basement that serves as the backstage for the biggest show in the world. Each guest who was shuttled through the basement and out an emergency exit was one more person who would not trample someone else or be trampled themselves. If our luck held, Mr. Arrezzo and Pete would be the only people to die in the park today.

Two deaths in one day. In a single morning. Mr. Arrezzo had expired over breakfast, and Pete had been flying the pre-noon show designed to welcome latecomers into the park. It was also timed to make the earlybirds stop in their tracks and wonder whether it wasn't time to grab an overpriced hot dog for lunch. The sooner they ate, the sooner the Corporation would have a chance to sell them another meal.

I pitied the PR chief. The Corporation does not appreciate publicity that can't be manipulated into a favorable slant. That's why they hired me. Good security does not make news. It is invisible. While my job application said all the right things—a degree in criminology, fifteen years of law enforcement experience, and specialized training in surveillance technology—my interview won me the job.

My employers have a deep and abiding knowledge of psychology. If you doubt that, spend a week at the park sometime. Ride all the rides once for pleasure, then ride them again for understanding. Watch how they use costumed characters and mildly humorous films to distract you from the fact that you just spent half-an-hour standing in line outdoors.

In Florida.

In August.

Then ride all the rides again. Make an effort *not* to look where they want you to look. Ignore the charming dolls chanting about how small the world is, and look for the underwater tracks that branch off from the ride's main line.

Where do you think they go? To a maintenance area, of course. When some destructive kid carves his name in a boat's shiny finish, somebody's got to hustle that water-craft to the repair shop. Maintaining the illusion of magical perfection is tough when 70,000 imperfect human beings troop through the park on any given day.

Now, ride something else and look for tell-tale gaps in the scenery where a door might hide. If some idiot stomps on your daughter's finger while they're clambering into one of those fake mine cars, do you think they're going to let you carry her, screaming and crying and bleeding, out the front entrance in front of all those waiting guests? Nope, they'll send a cast member to spirit your whole family away through a hidden exit, down into the base-ment where you'll find a friendly nurse with a first-aid kit and a lollipop for your young one. Hell, they might even send a dwarf to the emergency station to apply the antibiotic ointment.

My point is this: I've never personally met a colleague who admitted to being a psychologist, but I'm convinced the Corporation employs a whole staff of folks whose sole purpose is to keep 70,000 people happy every day. (I wish somebody would turn them loose in the Middle East. We might achieve peace in our time.)

I am convinced that those psychologists are intimately involved in the hiring process, and I believe that is why I was hired for this job. I am a man of utmost discretion. I consider the ramifications of my words and my actions. If anyone is less likely to say something stupid to the press or to a law enforcement official, I don't know who that person might be. I communicated that quality to my inter-viewers five years ago, and I was rewarded with my dream job. Two rather theatrical deaths made today a more difficult day than most, but I love my work. I knew I could handle this.

I backed up the surveillance video and took a close look at Peter Pan's final flight. He'd paused on the specially built balcony high up the castle's tallest tower, swashing and buckling with his faux sword until the crowd noticed him, then he'd launched himself into his trademark tumbling dive.

Guests have thrilled to Tinkerbell's nightly flight for decades, but there are stunts that only a male body can do. When the park added a second circus-trained aerialist to the lineup, the official website lit up with messages from awe-struck guests describing Peter Pan's daring entrance, so Pete the Aerialist became a permanent part of each day's entertainment...

...until tonight, when his flashy dive accelerated downward toward the point at which the safety cable should have pulled taut, yanking him out of gravity's grip. Only it didn't.

Perfectly toned arms and legs flailed at the air, trying to save an acrobat's body that could do nearly everything except fly. He landed on a paved area amid bushes and shadows that obscured my view, and I was glad for that. I had never liked Peter Pan's alter ego, a bitchy egotist whose real name was Merrill Chatham, but that didn't mean I was anxious for a look at his broken body. I would get a look at Merrill's remains soon enough, as well as a blow-by-blow description of the autopsy, but I was in no hurry.

I buzzed my assistant Keith. "Get everyone on my staff who's not working crowd control in here. Tell them to sift through every second of surveillance video of the castle's exterior and interior, starting just after Merrill's flight last night. If someone cut that cable, we should have it on video."

"We've already got all available staff here, running through the videos and trying to re-trace Mr. Arrezzo's last few hours."

Pulling my cell phone out of my pocket and heading for the door into the makeshift workroom where all those people were, I said, "I knew that. Watching Merrill die just got me rattled. Tell them to keep an eye out for him, too, while they're scanning the video. I want to know everything he did today, and that includes what time he took his last piss. Call in some off-duty staff to go through the castle videos, if that's what it takes."

Letting the door slam behind me, I dialed James, the person most likely to know things about the dead Peter Pan that no surveillance camera could ever pick up.

"James—" He cut me off before I got any further.

"You're calling me during working hours—" James took a breath and I knew he was checking his Caller ID. "—and you're on your company cell phone. Is that completely safe?"

"Please don't start. This is not the time. Merrill is dead."

"Dead? Merrill? He's the healthiest man I know. *God.* And you're calling me on your company phone, so I'm guessing he died in the park on your watch. Whatever happened?"

Striding through the broad underground corridors alongside staffers muttering amongst themselves about Peter Pan's fall, I wished I'd made this call before leaving my office. Reaching the infirmary where Merrill's body would be brought, I told James to hold on a second and stepped into an empty examining room, closing the door.

"He fell. His wire broke. We're trying to find out whether it was an accident. Can you tell me whether he had any enemies?"

"How should I know? What makes you think I knew anything about Merrill's friends or enemies? We had absolutely nothing in common. Other than being flaming faggots."

"The dressing room, James. Please don't make this into something it's not. I just thought you might know something about his personal life because you see him every day in the dancers' dressing room."

"Well, it *is* the single-gender Peyton Place of central Florida," James purred. The prospect of being asked to gossip on the company payroll had driven the knowledge that he was angry with me clean out of his mind. "Merrill cheats on Aaron quite regularly, and he flaunts it in his face, too."

"Would Aaron have killed him for it?"

"Sweetheart, that dressing room is filled right up every day with men that could just kill Merrill. First, there's Aaron. Then, there's all the other men he's loved and left. Also, he's stolen a few boyfriends from a few people who don't like him much any more. And don't forget the classic culprit, his understudy...me. How far do you think I might go for a chance at that job, not to mention the glory and the money that come with it?"

"James, be serious. You? A murderer? Who stomps the palmetto bugs at our house?"

"Well, you do. But I like palmetto bugs more than I liked Merrill."

I shifted the cell phone to my other ear. "So you're telling me that every male dancer in the park had some reason to want Merrill dead?"

"Pretty much. Any more questions? Want to know what I'm cooking for dinner?"

"I don't think I'll be home for dinner tonight."

❖ ◆ ❖ ◆ ❖

My professional observation of Merrill's body was much more unpleasant than viewing Mr. Arezzo's body had been. The Mafia chief had simply been a middle-aged man, limp and pale. The apple strudel smeared on his blank face had impaired his dignity, but it had not destroyed it.

Merrill, on the other hand...well, I happen to believe that God never intended a man to die with his green, pointy-toed boots on. And He damn sure didn't mean for him to do it in sparkly tights.

Merrill's broken body had nothing to tell me. All I needed was the identity of the person who sabotaged his cable. And I knew now that it *was* sabotage. My people had examined both ends of the cable. A clean cut had extended almost all the way through its diameter, leaving just enough material to hold the thing together, but not enough to support Merrill's weight.

This was murder.

I moved through the emergency center, peering first over one shoulder, then another.

"Anybody got anything?" I asked.

Keith caught up with my frenetic pacing long enough to say, "We've got nothing on who cut Merrill's cable. There's no security camera up there." *Of course there isn't,* I reflected. *Why would there be?*

A young blonde woman whose name had escaped me beckoned. "Mr. Arrezzo seems to have been...difficult. I've got video of him arguing with his wife, browbeating a ride attendant, yelling at his kids. And the park was only open two hours before he died. Who brings their kids someplace like this, then makes them cry?"

I didn't think his kids put rat poison in his strudel, and I told her so.

"Yeah, well, if I was married to a guy like that, I just might," the blonde confessed. "I mean, how easy could it be to divorce the Godfather?"

I nodded to concede her point. "See if you can get video of her poisoning the Godfather."

Another staffer tapped me on the shoulder and beckoned for me to lean down close. "Better have somebody check her work," he whispered. "Sounds to me like she might not mind if Mrs. Arrezzo got away with poisoning the man."

Another good point.

"Does anybody have the Arrezzos ordering their breakfast? I want as good a look at his food as we can get."

The blonde had the video I wanted. The victim ordered for his whole family, like a man who was accustomed to doing all the talking in his world. He got bacon and eggs and orange juice for everybody. Nobody got strudel but him, which might have been yet more evidence of his extreme self-centeredness. Or it could simply have meant that Mrs. Arrezzo was on a diet and the kids were holding out for ice cream later.

I couldn't see anything going in or on Mr. Arrezzo's food from the moment it was handed to him. There were gaps in camera coverage of the kitchen, but everything I could see looked good.

I wished the surveillance video had sound, but all I could see was the murder victim's mouth moving and his head nodding. In an hour, he'd be gone. For a while, I just watched the dead man talking.

Then I ran the tape again, trying to look at everything *but* the dead man. I scanned every face in the room, looking for Mafia hit men. All I saw were kids and diaper-bag-packing moms and a couple of dads dandling babies on their laps. Behind Mr. Arrezzo, surrounded by the restaurant's fake Bavarian trappings, his wife and kids cowered. In front of him, a teenaged cashier nervously hit the wrong keys on her register and had to start over. The dead man was not pleased.

Experience spoke in my ear, and it said, *Look beyond the immediate. Screen out the obvious. What else do you see?*

At the edge of the screen, I saw other teenaged cashiers, oblivious to the Arrezzos and their unfolding drama. And in the background, for just an instant, I saw Rosa.

❖ ◆ ❖ ◆ ❖

Beneath the park, there are dressing rooms and employee cafeterias and storage rooms and food staging facilities. There are broad passageways where golf carts shuttle people and things where they need to go. And if you stray far enough from the beaten path—if you burrow deep enough—you can find rooms full of things people have forgotten ever existed. In the case of Rosa, you can even find a person whose existence has faded from memory. Well, most memories.

The hardworking kids who run the park know Rosa. They see her pass quietly as they load the trains and serve the burgers and march in the parade. Some of them are afraid of her, but the ones with hearts see Rosa for what she is...a sweet-faced old lady with nowhere to go.

Rosa likes the kids. I've seen her walk past a little ticket-taker who was having a rough day and pat her on the elbow. No talking, no hugging, just a little pat. I'm not supposed to know this, but sometimes she fills in for them, spending a few minutes selling ice cream so that the ice cream guy can go to the bathroom or steal a moment with his girl. It's against the rules, but what the hell.

If old people are invisible in our world, then I guess you could say homeless old people inhabit some other dimension. You'd think Rosa would stand out in a crowd affluent enough to afford the park's hefty ticket prices. You'd think wrong. I've watched a family of five jostle past

Rosa as she stood leaning against a wall, minding her own business. Not one of them looked her in the face.

Can you imagine a better informant for someone in my position?

Rosa likes pizza, so I brought three slices down into the deepest part of the basement, to the storage closet she uses for an apartment. Kicking aside a sizeable stuffed pig with only one ear, I eased myself down onto a pile of stuff that she uses for a guest chair. As I did so, it occurred to me to wonder whether Rosa ever had any other guests but me.

She sat on another pile beside mine. At the bottom of her pile, I recognized a cast-off ballgown and a pirate suit. Rods hung on Rosa's walls at about eye level all around the room, suggesting that the space had once been used for costume storage. This would explain the air conditioning vent in the closet ceiling. Fabric gathers mildew within days in this climate, unless the humidity is wrung out of the air with expensive machinery.

Rosa seems to attract lost sweaters and misplaced stuffed animals. These things serve her well as clothing and furniture. As I looked around the room, it occurred to me that maybe we should pay her for being the park's scavenger. A teepee of old gardening tools leaning in the corner of the closet made me wonder whether Rosa ventured out at night to shape up the topiary bushes, just for fun.

"You've had a bad day," Rosa said, patting my elbow.

"You hear about Merrill?"

"A pity. He was a very pretty person." Her voice had the high, keening quaver of the very old.

"Did you know him?"

"He only talked to pretty people like himself."

Well, that was true. So I'd proceed on the assumption that Rosa knew Merrill.

"Rosa, did you know that another man died in the park today?"

"Yes." She smoothed a thin veil of gray hair away from her forehead. Her right eye was murky with an untreated cataract. "He was a gangster."

My, how well the employee grapevine functioned. Rosa probably knew more about Arrezzo's death than I did. But then, that was the reason I was here.

"What else do you know about him?"

"Only that he was the kind of man who would make his own children cry. *Here*. In this place that was built for children. They're better off without him."

That seemed a bit harsh, but Rosa's whole life was harsh, so I let it go.

"I know you were there when he died." This was a stretch. I only knew that Rosa was there when he bought his food, but I bent the truth and was rewarded with the effect I wanted. "What did you see?"

"It was a quiet thing. He twitched some and dropped his fork. His wife—she's a dainty little woman, don't you think?—looked up from her own plate and asked him what was wrong. Then he just...fell over."

"Did his wife help him serve his food? Did she salt it for him? Did she help him sugar his coffee?"

"He didn't have coffee." I knew this already. The fact that Rosa knew it, too, made her that much more credible as a witness. "I did hear him ask her for an antacid tablet."

"Did you see her give it to him?" I didn't have any tape of Mrs. Arrezzo passing a pill to her doomed husband, but that didn't mean it didn't happen.

"Nope. Didn't see anything like that."

She eyed my pizza crust. I gave it to her.

"Did you see anything else that will help me find out whether Mr. Arrezzo was murdered?"

"Only thing I saw after that was two crying kids. How are they holding up? Here. Take these to the man's children." She clutched the one-eared pig to her breast, as if it were too precious to give, and held out a toy car and a marionette with tangled strings instead. "Tell them that Rosa wants them to feel better."

I knew when I'd been dismissed.

I recognized the tap at my office door. It had been a long time since James had visited me at work, and he'd only done it once. I hadn't been sufficiently welcoming and he'd punished me for it for a week.

Discretion, circumspection, keeping one's own counsel —these are all ways of saying that I keep my business to myself. I don't chat about my home life around the water cooler, and I don't say stupid things about my employer to the press. This close-to-the-vest quality had won me my job, and it had lost me two lovers that I didn't want to lose. Two, so far. James had one foot out the door.

He tapped again, and I knew that he'd walked through the emergency headquarters outside my door, which was clotted with a half-dozen personnel whom I'd called in to work the two murder cases. Law enforcement types are not typically kind to men with James' flair for fashion. This was just one in a long list of reasons why I treasured my own circumspection. To be fair, I once knew an emphatically straight cop who took a bullet for the gay partner who had sat beside him in a squad car for years. Still, in a field where even the women are expected to be macho, the closet feels like a very safe place to me.

I heard no insults or catcalls through the door, but I imagined them. I hurried to open it and to let James in, where it was safe.

As soon as the door shut behind him, he burst out with his news, "You remember we were wondering about Aaron, whether he maybe killed Merrill out of jealousy? Well, he's gone. He quit! Said he couldn't face this place without his true love's presence or something like that."

When I took a second to respond, he kept talking, "Well, isn't that important? I was afraid someone would overhear me, so I came straight here to tell you."

Sometimes I think I just don't talk fast enough to suit James. Sometimes I think maybe I think too much to suit him, but I really was just gathering my thoughts. He interpreted my hesitation differently.

"I shouldn't have come here. You've never wanted me here, and I've respected that, but this is important. This is *murder* and you asked me to help. Well, I gave you the news. You do whatever you want with it."

He headed for the door and was nearly knocked to the floor by a half-dozen security officers bursting into my office.

"We've got video of Merrill fighting with a bunch of kids just before the park closed last night," Keith said, popping a jump drive into my office computer.

"And a couple of their dads," another guy added.

I was interested to hear it, but my eyes were on James' back as he worked his way through the maze of desks hauled in just for this emergency.

"Who in the hell is that?" Keith asked. A couple of the other guys tittered, but there were no crude jokes, no insinuations. Yet. They would come after James was out of earshot, and James knew it.

Through my half-open door, I could see him. His hand was on the doorknob that would take him out of sight. Forever.

Keith looked at me, waiting for the answer to his question.

Who in the hell is that?

Keith deserved an answer, and so did James. Maybe because I'd just had lunch with an old woman who lived alone in her closet, I knew the right answer.

"That, ladies and gentlemen," I said, glancing about the room with my customary air of command, "is the love of my life."

James heard me. I could tell. He continued, uninterrupted, in the smooth motion of opening a door. He made a grand exit, like the dancer that he is, but I thought he'd probably be back.

The answer to Merrill's death was indeed in the video Keith and his friend had found, though not in the way they expected. The night before, just after his last flight, Merrill had been the center of an ugly scene. His poisonous and cocky personality never took a rest, not even when he'd just been cheered by tens of thousands of adoring fans. As he walked away from his triumphant landing, he'd been besieged by children wanting autographs. Unfortunately, Merrill just hadn't been in the mood to do something nice for the people who paid his handsome salary.

When you're brushing off a few clinging kids, it can't be a surprise when one falls on his little diapered butt. And it can't come as much of a shock when his daddy tries to rip off your feathered cap and beat you with it.

I looked at my in-box, where the day's petty woes festered. I'd had time for nothing but these two murders, but I would lay odds that several guests had complained about Merrill's behavior and that those complaints were waiting for me right there.

"Back it up and slow it down," I barked. And I set myself the usual task of looking in the background for information that's hiding in plain sight.

None of the people watching the altercation looked familiar. It would have been too much to hope that the Arrezzos were standing there, waiting for me to tie the two murders up into a neat bow. Still, there was a smudge of pink on the ground that I thought I recognized.

Another run through the footage confirmed that this pink smudge was a stuffed pig with a missing ear. And a third pass showed me that the pink pig walked away from the scene, though obviously not under its own power.

The pig was there when Merrill started to misbehave, and it was gone when he regained his senses.

Rosa was there. And she didn't tell me.

Rosa didn't seem surprised to see me again so soon, and she didn't seem surprised to see that, for the first time in our acquaintance, I hadn't come alone.

In my office, my team was assembling the evidence. They already had the video that showed Rosa had been at arm's length from Mr. Arrezzo's food, just before he succumbed to rat poison—which was probably easily available down here in the vast network of storerooms where she lived. And now they had the video that linked Rosa to Merrill through the shabby little pig.

No record existed of Merrill's cable being cut, but surely one of the topiary shaping tools leaning in the corner of Rosa's room would have served that function well enough. I jerked my head in that direction, so that

Keith would know to gather the tools and find the one that had been scarred by cutting a metal cable. He had already deployed a team to search the area for an unguarded tray of rat poison. Or a tray where some rat poison had been.

Finding the right poison, as well as the scarred blades of a pair of tree loppers, would give me two pieces of physical evidence to shore up my flimsy web of circumstantial evidence. These things would show that Rosa had the means to do the crimes.

I had video confirmation that she'd had the opportunity to poison Mr. Arrezzo, but my cameras had not been conveniently arranged to capture her in the act of cutting Merrill's cable. I had a few seconds showing just a glimpse of her from behind, standing near the employee entrance to a web of backstage corridors, one of which led out onto the deadly castle balcony. It wasn't enough.

Can you imagine the publicity that a trial over the murder of Peter Pan would produce? I needed an open-and-shut case.

It was going to be hard to get a jury to render judgment on a murder case, merely by showing that the suspect and her pink pig had been present the last time the glitter-sprinkled victim had behaved like a diva, drunk on a testosterone-spiked cocktail. Still, the Corporation didn't hire me just for my law enforcement prowess. Their psychologists had determined that I was psychologically right for the job. I won my position because I choose my words carefully, and because I think through the full ramifications of my every action, and because I'm a very passable amateur psychologist myself.

I understood exactly what had driven Rosa to kill, and I knew I could make her tell me about it.

"I know why you live here, Rosa."

Rather than meet my eyes, she looked at her hands clasped tightly together in her lap. Every joint was swollen to the point that her fingers canted in odd directions. "I live here because it's warm all the year. When you've got no roof and no hope of a roof, Florida looks mighty good."

"That's true, but it's not what I meant. I meant that I know why you live here at the park."

"I do have a nice place here," she said, as her good eye wandered up toward the air conditioning vent. "Cool in the summer. Warm in the winter. The bathroom's right down the hall."

"That's still not what I meant, and you know it." Finally, the rheumy eyes rested on my face, so I delivered the key to her crime. "This is a very special place."

"I like happiness," she said dreamily, looking upward toward the park that rested on the ground above our heads. "If I want to see people smiling, all I have to do is go up top. There's sunshine up there, too, but I need happiness more than sunshine."

"And children?"

"I need children more than anything. Here, I can see happy children all the time." Her eyes drifted down to the damaged pig. "The children...the ones whose father made them cry. Did you give them the toys I sent?"

I nodded.

"Because, if you didn't, they can have this one."

I wanted to say, *They're crying now. You made them cry, Rosa,* but that would have been too much for her. It would have cost me my confession. Instead, I said, "You worked hard today for the children. Are you very tired?"

"Oh, no!" Her voice was almost youthful, rich and musical. "Oh, nothing is hard when you do it for children. I could run so fast today because I knew I had to. If I'd been slow, I would have missed my chance at the gangster's food, but I got back with the rat bait just fast enough. After that, I felt so strong. I knew I could pick the right tool and carry it up to the balcony. I knew I'd be able to balance out there long enough to do what needed doing."

"And these things needed doing to Mr. Arrezzo and Merrill because..."

"Because they made the children cry. And they did it here! This place is...well, it's like sacred ground. You leave your tears outside. Everybody needs a place like that. And now those children can have it." A pale flush spread over her withered cheeks. "They can have it because of me. I gave it back to them."

I had my confession, but I wasn't sure whether I was proud of it.

The Corporation avoids bad publicity with all its hefty financial might, and I can't say I blame them. They've never asked me to lie for them, and there's no sin that I can see in putting the truth in its best possible light. And, as Rosa has finally made me see, the Corporation exists for the purpose of giving people pleasure. Particularly the very small people who are supremely unimportant everywhere else in the world.

The details of Rosa's conviction, other than the bare facts, never made the press. The public was told that Mr. Arezzo and Merrill Chatham were killed by a deranged guest who had been put away in a facility from which she can never expect to emerge. This is true, and this is all they need to know.

The Corporation was exceedingly grateful for my speed and, as always, for my discretion in solving these crimes. It has shown its gratitude in monetary terms. There also have been quiet assurances that any inappropriate behavior in the workplace toward James, me, or the two of us as a family unit will trigger prompt action. A woman even came to my office to ask me, and I quote, "Is there anything else that the Corporation can do for you?"

I described to them a place that was warm and safe. A place where a criminally insane elderly woman would feel as if she'd been transported to a resort. A place where people would smile when they spoke to her. A place where she could play cards with other peaceful but criminally insane people, blissfully unaware that there were armed guards watching every moment of her well-earned retirement.

Perhaps it was too much to hope that children could be brought to visit now and then. I wanted Rosa to be put in a place where she was so happy that she'd never notice that there were locks on the doors.

From the look on the woman's face, I knew that the Corporation owned just the right place for Rosa. Or it would soon. After all, it does specialize in building places where the impossible seems real and dreams come true.

My uncle helped build the real theme park in central Florida that features a very tall castle, and he worked there for more than twenty years. I've ridden every ride in the shadow of that castle many times. Even now, when I take a child to experience the very same things I did as a child, I feel a sense of nostalgia that's hard to explain.

When I was sixteen, I began talking about studying engineering in college, so my uncle arranged for me to visit the parts of the park where tourists don't go. I saw the chillers that made cold water so that those vast buildings could be air conditioned. I saw the building where they made all those hamburgers and sent them to the snack stands in the park. I even got to walk through the famous basement, acres in size, that supports the mammoth operation above it. The logistics involved in making tens of thousands of people happy, every single day, were mindboggling.

Once I'd emerged from the basement through a gate that I'd seen many times, but never noticed, I started noticing other things—barely noticeable doors and stealthy employees who were very good at cleaning up the garbage left behind, every day, by a crowd of guests the size of a small city. When you've seen all the magic a hundred times, it's much easier to look through the magic and see how it's done, and I think you get a certain insight into the people who bring the magic to life. That insight was the genesis of the nameless narrator of "Mouse House."

It often happens that I begin a story, only to find that the character and I have a different idea of what the story is about. I did not know that the viewpoint character of "Mouse House" was gay until he said so, but once he made that revelation, I knew it was the key to the story I want to tell. Of course, a gay man whose profession requires him to be utterly circumspect is going to be comfortable in the closet...almost comfortable...sort of comfortable...but this aspect of his personality is going to be hell on the man who shares his life. This realization helped me give his character a depth that makes me like him a lot, flaws and all.

Maybe I need to bring him back in another story. Hmmm...I could throw somebody off a monorail...

– Mary Anna

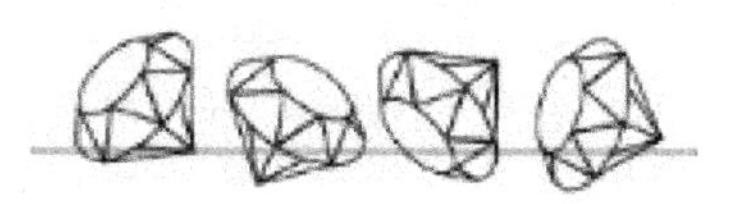

STARCH

I placed this story back-to-back with "Mouse House" for a fairly straightforward reason. In both these stories, I came to feel that I was dictating the personal life of a very strong character who was whispering a story in my ear. In both cases, the viewpoint characters told me almost immediately that they were gay, although I had not known it when I sat down to write. And in both cases, the narrator's sexual orientation and life experience made the narrative take a different course than it might otherwise have. As a writer, I love the feeling that a story has unfolded in the only possible way that it can.

Meet Nurse Crain. If you are ever deeply anesthetized while in the same room with a murderer, she is the kind of person you should hope is watching over you.

– Mary Anna

STARCH

by Mary Anna Evans and Lillian Sellers

In 1954, the word "nurse" was a female one. We worked among women. We were taught by women. We trained at an all-female school that required us to live on-campus—with women, of course. It was an odd time and place to be a lesbian, and this was particularly true for me. I had, at that time, never even heard the word "lesbian," and thus had no idea that I was one.

In those days, on-duty nurses were addressed by their last names, so I was known as "Crain." I liked the notion of dispensing with "Mrs." and "Miss," and all the social baggage that separated women outside the hospital into single girls, married ladies, and old maids. The doctors we served were, without exception, male, and we were expected to stand when any of them entered the room, just as gentlemen outside the hospital rose out of respect for ladies. I positively reveled in this perversion of the prevailing custom. If anyone was ever born to be a nurse, I was.

I loved the uniform, white and severe. I kept mine starched so stiff that the collar chafed at my neck. Even our caps were starched to the texture of cardboard. My dark hair was no longer lank when I pinned it up beneath that old-style cap. Its medieval lines suited my strong features and, while I was still not pretty when I wore it, I was surely memorable.

Only one thing could have made me give up my cherished whites. When I was offered a job as a surgical nurse in the OR, I accepted on the spot, even though it meant that my working life would be spent in a nondescript scrub dress. Surgery is a life-or-death proposition, every day. This job was a chance to make people well, every day. People that might have died would roll out of my OR into decades of life. Every day.

How could I turn that down? I spent the rest of my career in the OR.

And that is how I found myself face-to-face with bloody, messy, intentional death.

Murder.

I was the circulating nurse that night, which meant that my entire purpose for breathing was to make sure that nothing went wrong. When a surgeon or a scrub nurse or an anesthesiologist needed an instrument unexpectedly, the circulating nurse had better by God get it for them. If she was good, she knew what her doctors needed before they did.

I was good.

It was an emergency case, a terrible one, the kind of case you remember forever. A twenty-five-year-old woman, more than eight months pregnant, had gone to sleep at the wheel and drifted off the road. Her car rolled twice before slamming into a telephone pole. If you're old enough to remember 1954, then you already know the worst part. She wasn't wearing a seatbelt.

I don't like to think about how many times that poor woman's body must have slammed into the car door or the steering wheel or the stick shift or the roof of that car. And every impact inflicted its damage.

There were no paramedics in those days, simply attendants who loaded the wounded into ambulances and ferried them to the hospital. There were no cell phones, either, so those attendants couldn't call ahead and warn the hospital what to expect. But in serious cases, and this one was serious, the policeman on the scene used his radio to pass along the bad news. Thanks to that alert lawman, an emergency surgical team began assembling before the patient ever reached the hospital.

I was at home washing my supper dishes when I got the emergency call, but barely ten minutes passed before I parked my car in the hospital lot and hit the ground running.

The nursing supervisor met me in the surgical dressing room, briefing me as I peeled off my street clothes and pulled on a clean scrub dress.

"All the other on-call staff were in the hospital when we got the message, so you're the last to arrive. I've helped Moseley suit up. The room is ready and the patient is prepped, so we're all set."

"What's her condition?"

"Head injuries. Multiple broken bones. Internal bleeding. She's comatose, so Dr. Gomez intubated her in the ER to keep her from aspirating during surgery."

"So what are we going to fix first?"

"First, we're going to take the baby. The patient's thirty-five weeks along. I'd say the baby's got a lot better chance than she does."

It made sense. Cesarean sections were performed with lightning speed in those days. Once the patient was anesthetized, the goal was to deliver the child within a minute and a half, before the sleep-inducing chemicals could make their way from the mother's blood to the baby's. Otherwise, the risk of damage to the child was too great.

Waiting ninety seconds to begin repairing her internal injuries posed no great risk to the patient, not compared to the damage that had already been done. And in the process, we would save a life.

Rushing into the OR, I noticed that Dr. Lacey was scrubbed up and ready to assist, even though I was sure that Dr. Wilkinson had been on call. Displaying the clair-voyant talents of a true nurse, the supervisor leaned toward me and whispered, "Dr. Wilkinson was supposed to be in the hospital, but...well, he couldn't be found. Dr. Lacey was here, so we drafted him."

This did not bode well for Dr. Wilkinson. He was widely known as a man devoted to ethanol and to other men's wives, but he was a competent doctor. The other surgeons tended to overlook foibles of such a manly nature, so long as patient care wasn't compromised. Failing to respond to an emergency call, however, was an intolerable offense, even for the old boys' network.

The surgeon, Dr. Hale, was scrubbed up and ready to get started. Dr. Auburn, the pediatrician who would take charge of the baby, stood with his arms crossed and his head cocked awkwardly, as if he knew that he was useless until his patient was born.

Moseley was laying out the instruments directly on the patient's draped thigh, where Dr. Hale liked them. Dr. Lacey stood across from her, watching to make sure she did it right. This served only to make Moseley nervous.

Doctors can smell fear, just as easily as wild beasts can. They had savaged her daily during her first months on the job, until I took her aside and showed her a few tricks, like how to clip sutures with her left hand. It helps to be ambidextrous when you're working in quarters as con-fined as a human body cavity, and not all surgeons are good with their non-dominant hand. When they see you do something that they can't, they're impressed. And when they're impressed, they tend to shut up and leave you alone.

Dr. Gomez had moved his rolling equipment chest to its place next to the patient's head. He was as finicky about his anesthesiology equipment as any of the surgeons were about their tools, and the patient's life rested in his hands just as certainly as it did in theirs. It's well-known among nurses that people who choose to be surgeons or anesthesiologists have total confidence in their own god-like powers. This does not make them pleasant people.

Having known perhaps a hundred surgeons in my working life, I have developed a most sincere sympathy for their spouses. While it was a shock to find Dr. Wilkinson dead in the supply closet—actually, he was dead all over the supply closet—in retrospect, it was not surprising that someone hated him enough to kill him. He was a surgeon.

I only stepped into the supply closet to fetch a retractor to replace one that Dr. Lacey had dropped. Retractors were hardly necessary for a C-section, since the overstuffed uterus rises out of the abdomen as soon as it's opened, making itself easily accessible without mechanical aid. No, retractors would be helpful later in the evening, when we were looking for the bone fragments and punctured organs that might well kill this young woman.

As expected, I found the supply room well-stocked with sterile retractors. People who supply operating rooms believe in planning ahead. Unexpected events kill patients, so redundancy is a cardinal virtue. On the other hand, the closet's ample supply of surgical tools hadn't been such a good thing for Dr. Wilkinson. Someone had used a scalpel to send him to his Maker. I studied the wreckage of his body with a detachment born of years spent watching bodies being cut apart and sewn back together.

His throat had been slit, severing the trachea and depriving him of the ability to breathe or to cry for help. Then, not satisfied with merely ending his life, the murderer had enjoyed a moment of recreational surgery. Using the same vertical incision that Dr. Hale would soon use to deliver a baby, the killer had opened Dr. Wilkinson' abdomen and festooned the supply closet with his entrails. I assessed the volume of blood splashed about and judged that this had been done quickly, before his heart stopped beating.

I remember thinking that it would have been a damn sight neater if the murderer had just taken a gun and shot him.

A good nurse pays attention to detail. The lone surgical gown in the hamper next to the door was saturated with blood that was too red. It had been more than three hours since the last patient was wheeled out of this OR, so the freshly soiled gown was the one that the killer had used to fend off Dr. Wilkinson' blood. If the killer had dropped scrubs into the hamper, I would have known the killer's gender, because we women wore scrub dresses in those days. Unfortunately, surgical gowns were unisex.

I couldn't even glean any information from the gown's size, since surgical gowns were one-size-fits-all. At least in theory. In reality, they fit the doctors quite well. Being a tall, raw-boned woman, I too found them comfortable, but they hung like sacks on the smaller nurses.

An empty cloth wrapper tossed into the hamper with the bloody gown told me that someone had opened a sterile gown, either in preparation for premeditated murder or as a replacement for the clean gown they'd worn into the room. The supply closet had never seemed a particularly threatening place before I realized that it was kept stocked with a wide variety of murder weapons, stored alongside a stack of clothing specially designed to protect one's clothing from spurting blood.

Other than the surgical gown and the empty bag, nothing else in my supply closet was out of place. Well, except for Dr. Wilkinson and his entrails.

I devoted a moment to his injuries. The scalpel had been wielded by a steady hand, with no hacking or jabbing. Because the abdominal incision had been done hastily, nicking the intestines in a couple of places, I couldn't say for sure that it had been done by a surgeon. Still, if the murderer didn't wield a scalpel for a living, I was willing to bet that he or she had watched someone else do it, time and again. I knew a couple of dozen people personally who could have done it, but my circle of friends has always been somewhat atypical.

I backed out of the supply closet and into the OR. Though I'd been with the body hardly a minute and I'd touched nothing, I felt as soiled as if I had lain down and rolled in Dr. Wilkinson' blood. If one of the five people gathered around the unconscious patient had looked up, my face would have told them something was terribly wrong, but they didn't. The operation was beginning.

I lingered near the supply closet door, outside the imaginary line that delineated the "sterile field," the portion of the OR where exacting techniques protected the patient from the infectious organisms that we all carry around with us. The five people inside the sterile field were intent on their work.

The patient's body was swathed in drapes, with only her pale and bulbous belly exposed. The anesthesiologist had done his job, so the baby needed to come out right away. After that, the woman lying unconscious on the table needed life-saving surgery, immediately. Could I afford to wait until both patients were stable before I let someone know there was a killer loose in the hospital?

I pictured a killer walking down the second-floor corridor, pushing open the double doors labeled, "Surgical Suite—Authorized Personnel Only" and walking in. It had been four hours since the seven-to-three shift had completed the last case of the day and gone home, but that didn't mean the surgical wing had been deserted all that time. After hours, the cleaning staff carted dirty gowns to the laundry. They washed bloody surgical instruments and took them to Central Supply for sterilization. They restocked the supply closets with freshly sterilized gowns and instruments.

People don't just walk off the street and decide to take a tour of a hospital's operating rooms. Maybe the killer was lucky enough to slip in without being seen, but I doubted it. It seemed more likely that Dr. Wilkinson was slain by someone he expected to see, someone who walked past the cleaning staff unnoticed. Suddenly, I saw the five people surrounding an unconscious mother-to-be in a more sinister light. The nursing supervisor had explicitly said that they'd all been in the hospital when the emergency call came in. Any one of them could have ripped Dr. Wilkinson's guts out.

I looked at Dr. Gomez, rhythmically squeezing the bag delivering cyclopropane and oxygen to the patient. His hands would breathe for her until she was able to breathe again on her own. The sweat beads gathering on his brow didn't indicate guilt. They didn't indicate innocence, either, only that his job was both physically and mentally strenuous.

Dr. Auburn, as a pediatrician, didn't ordinarily frequent the OR, so I ignored him for the time being.

Dr. Lacey stood on the far side of the patient, ready to assist Dr. Hale. His expression was impassive, just as it was during surgeries that ended in amputation or a diagnosis of terminal cancer. Poker players and murderers could learn many a lesson in control by studying surgeons.

Moseley stood on the far side of the patient, nervously counting the sponges arrayed on the tray beside her.

Dr. Hale stood with his back to me, scalpel in hand, preparing to open a woman's body. There was nothing, no twitching shoulders, no trembling legs, nothing that might have told me whether he knew that Dr. Wilkinson lay dead behind the door I had just closed.

He sliced into the patient's abdomen, and the first bead of blood extended in the wake of his scalpel into a fine, straight, red line. Dr. Lacey went to work sponging the wound and clamping bleeders, and Moseley began a gallant effort to keep up with his and Dr. Hale's demand for hemostats and scissors and clamps.

Mentally urging her to use both hands like I'd taught her, I left Moseley to her bumbling and tried to think. Would someone have planned to kill a man in a supply closet with a single door that opened into an operating room, which also offered a single door and, thus, only one escape route? Not if they possessed even a particle of good sense, and I didn't know any dummies who could handle a scalpel the way Dr. Wilkinson's murderer did.

Dr. Hale's scalpel sliced through another layer of the patient's body, opening up the abdominal wall. Dr. Lacey and Moseley hurried to clamp another crop of bleeders. Dr. Auburn took a step forward, anxious to meet his patient. Dr. Gomez just kept pumping gas.

Who would want to kill Dr. Wilkinson? I don't ordinarily speak ill of the dead, but the man had built a collection of well-deserved enemies. As I've said, surgeons are not known for their pleasant personalities. Only the day before, Dr. Wilkinson had lost a patient while Dr. Lacey assisted. He'd laid the blame squarely at Dr. Lacey's feet, claiming that the younger doctor's choice of the wrong retractor had hampered his surgical skill, directly causing the patient's death. I know this, even though the argument took place in the physicians' private lounge, because their voices were clearly audible to everyone within three counties.

Moseley, on the other hand, had rarely been the butt of the dead doctor's wrath, despite her incessant fumbling, probably because she was widely believed to be sleeping with him. Given that she'd been caught in a linen closet with Dr. Gomez, and that she'd been named as a party to Dr. Auburn's divorce, I was inclined to believe the hospital's formidable army of gossips.

Lovers' quarrels had ended in murder before, though I had trouble picturing ineffectual little Moseley yanking her victim's intestines out. It was just as plausible to think that Dr. Gomez or Dr. Auburn had killed his rival out of jealousy.

And, while on the topic of jealousy, the hospital grapevine said that ice-cool Dr. Hale had been heard to swear a long string of oaths involving God, the devil, and somebody's mother, when Dr. Wilkinson was honored for developing a new technique for gall bladder removal. I'd watched Dr. Hale use that technique for years, but he'd been too busy taking care of patients to bother writing a scholarly paper.

Was he capable of murder? Well, he was a surgeon. Playing God on a daily basis might give a man a penchant for holy retribution.

The brilliant overhead lights bleached the color from the room. The surgical team's caps and masks obscured their faces, leaving only their eyes visible. Were any of them hoping to bluff themselves out of a murder charge? Was there enough evidence left in the supply closet to convict anyone?

The lights reflected off their hair, their clothes, their eyes, the cloths draping the patient's body. Everything was thrown into a black-and-white world of light and darkness. The shadows at their feet were night-black, as if the floor had dissolved beneath them and exposed the shallower regions of hell. The living red of the patient's blood was the only color in the room.

A scalpel was poised above the patient's exposed uterus, and its surface rippled with the baby's last languid movements before emerging into life's stark light. I couldn't stand by, leaving the care of a mother and her child to a killer. I studied them again, one by one, and it struck me that everyone in the room knew that I'd just come out of the supply closet. If the murderer was present, he or she knew what I'd seen.

Dr. Hale reached into the incision for the baby. Dr. Lacey cursed Moseley for being slow with a clamp, because she still insisted on doing everything with her right hand. This puzzled me, because she knew better, until I noticed her left hand hanging curled and useless by her side. It occurred to me that it was dangerous for a married man to carry on with a jittery woman who knew how to open up his trachea.

How would a short woman slice the throat of a taller man? A right-handed woman would stand behind him, reach up and grab his chin with her left hand to pull him down toward her, then bring her right hand up to cut from left to right. A clumsy woman might also accidentally deliver a pretty good slash to her left hand.

I raised my eyes from a rubber glove that could well be hiding some damning evidence and saw that Moseley had taken her eyes off the patient. She studied me for a bare second, then took her second deadly action of the day.

Using her good hand, she released a hemostat, allowing a major blood vessel to hemorrhage into the patient's abdomen. While both surgeons rushed to salvage this disaster, Moseley grabbed a scalpel and stepped around the foot of the operating table, toward the door on the far side of the room from me. Then she passed the door, hurrying toward the patient's head.

Why is she moving away from the door? I wondered, but only for a second, until Moseley lashed out and slashed through the hose delivering oxygen to the patient. Dr. Gomez dived for his rolling supply chest, but she kicked it across the room, forcing another person to choose between chasing her and saving the patient. I was on the wrong side of the operating table. She could be out the door, fleeing into the hospital's maze of corridors, before I reached her.

Perhaps our minds were traveling down those corridors together. At precisely the moment when I realized she was going to need a hostage to get out of the hospital, she took one.

Wrapping her left arm around Dr. Auburn's waist, she reached up and pressed the scalpel to his throat, saying, "If anybody follows me out of here, he dies."

The brilliant lights illuminated three doctors doing what they did best. Dr. Lacey was stanching the bleeding of a patient in critical danger, Dr. Gomez was doing his damndest to restore her air supply, and Dr. Hale was trying to free a baby from a haven that had turned deadly. There was nobody to stop Moseley but me.

I had chosen to put myself in the middle of emergency situations every day of my working life. That was what *I* did best. I did not intend to stand by, helpless, and watch this one unfold.

Stretching my gangly legs to their full length, I leapt onto the operating table and stood astride the patient, one sensible white shoe on either side of her chest. It was the only time in my life that I knowingly violated a sterile field. I stood there for an instant, probably dropping germs and skin particles into the patient's open incision, then I launched myself onto Moseley. Her scalpel-wielding hand released Dr. Auburn to deal with the more immediate threat.

Me.

She did her best with the scalpel, carving a slice through my tibialis anterior, but she couldn't reach anything but my leg before I descended on her, feet first. Her left clavicle broke under my right foot, and my left foot took out a couple of her ribs.

I presume that the police made sure she got adequate medical care, but I can assure you that she wasn't treated by anybody at our hospital. The police didn't trust us.

❖ ◆ ❖ ◆ ❖

Later in the day, when my leg wound had been repaired and I was resting in my hospital room, an aide from the nursery walked in with a wheelchair. Settling me into it, she said, "The baby's mother is…um…not able to visit with her. Nobody knows where the father is. We thought you'd like to get to know her."

I passed the afternoon and the evening in a rocking chair with the unnamed baby girl. When word of her mother's condition filtered through the hospital grapevine, we all knew that there would be no sweet mother-daughter moments for a long time, maybe never. After all these years, I guess there's no harm in saying that the nursery staff brought her to my room for any number of unauthorized visits, hospital regulations be damned.

A couple of weeks later, the baby's gutless father surfaced, staying in town just long enough to name the baby Rachel and to saddle his mother with Rachel and her older sister. He committed his wife to a place where she would get lifelong care, courtesy of the state's taxpayers, and I guess that was a good thing. Nothing was going to repair the damage wrought by too much lost blood and too many minutes without oxygen. I trust that she got better care in that institution than he would have given her.

A hospital houses many eyes, and there was always someone anxious to tell me when they'd seen Rachel at church, or at their child's piano recital, or on the playground. Sometimes I saw her myself, perched in the basket of her grandmother's grocery cart. In time, I gleaned information from the newspaper which, in a small town, is always happy to report the exploits of a star basketball player or the awards granted to a talented student. It has been a quarter-century since Rachel married and moved away, but I still hear about her now and then.

My life has been long and productive, filled with the work I love and graced by good friends. There have been no lovers and no natural children, but I have not minded that so very much, because once I had a baby. Her name is Rachel, and she became a grandmother a year ago last March. She is fifty years old today.

My mother was an operating room nurse in the 1950s. The stories she told me when I was a little girl played a huge part in the genesis of "Starch." The other thing that prompted this story was very simple: Anthony Neil Smith, the editor of the well-respected noir publication Plots with Guns, *asked me for a story.*

Let me put this into context. I spent most of my twenties writing short stories that were never published. They received kind and complimentary rejections from many editors, some of them quite famous, but there is no denying the fact that nobody ever bought one.

Artifacts *was published in 2003 and I attended my first mystery conference that spring, Mayhem in the Midlands, where this middle-aged mother of three inexplicably found herself hanging out with a bunch of younger guys who wrote in the darkest, grittiest, hippest genre of them all, noir. One of them was Anthony Neil Smith. Later that year, I bumped into Neil at the World Mystery Convention, better known as*

Bouchercon, and he said he'd enjoyed reading Artifacts. *Would I like to write a story for* Plots with Guns*?*

Would I? Of course I would. Finally (finally!), I was going to sell a short story after having tried for so many years that I was beginning to question my own sanity. Unfortunately, I needed to express a teeny tiny concern.

"Um...Neil? I don't write noir."

He told me not to fear. Plots with Guns *had only one rule: a gun must be mentioned somewhere in the narrative. He even gave me a helpful suggestion.*

"Have Faye dig up a musket."

Well, I wanted to step outside my comfort zone a little more than that, but I tend to associate noir fiction with a good bit of gore, and I get a little queasy just thinking about such things. How was I going to come up with a story that featured blood and guts?

Suddenly, my mother's surgical stories popped into my mind, and I knew that an operating room could be the genesis of a very different locked-room mystery. I conferred with her by phone to get the layout of the OR back in those days. She told me more first-hand stories than my delicate stomach really wanted to hear. She even mailed me some of her old textbooks. In the end, she was so much help that I credited her as co-author, so if you Google her name and Confessions of an Idiosyncratic Mind, you'll see that Sarah Weinman called our story "twisted."

My children are so proud.

Despite the fact that the murder and attempted murder in this story were committed with scalpels and the misuse of medical equipment, I did manage to comply with Neil's request that I at least mention a gun. (How else could he explain why he accepted it for a publication called Plots with Guns*?)*

Did you see the gun? If not, look back and see how long it takes you to find it.

Mama passed away last year, and I'm very glad that she got a chance to see our story go out into the world.

– Mary Anna

THE LAST RADICAL

I've known Libby Hellmann since our first books came out. We've done a book tour together. We were nominated for the same award. We've commiserated about business highs and lows. More pertinent to the discussion here, I think she's a hell of a good writer.

Putting together my own anthology gives me the opportunity to give my readers something extra that they might not get any other way. As you've seen, I have the freedom to mix essays in amongst my short stories, and I can give you an excerpt from a novel that is important to me. I can and did, as you shall see, tell you about a short story that was the genesis for a published and award winning novel, then extract that story from the original text and show it to you. And I can include the work of other writers I respect.

I hope you enjoy Libby's story. I did. And don't miss her new 5-star-reviewed police procedural thriller, TOXICITY.

THE LAST RADICAL

by Libby Hellmann

Soft explosions of flame crackled and licked the side of the grill. The tang of charred meat filled the air. I edged closer, prepared to supervise, but when David, who had taken over chef's duties, spotted me, he raised his eyebrows and lowered his chin, his way of warning me to back off. I picked up the Merlot and refilled my guests' glasses.

"Ellie, I shouldn't." Jamie covered her glass with her hand. My neighbors, Jamie and Ted Matheson, were over for dinner with their son Conrad.

"Nonsense," I said. "This could be the last barbecue of the season. We'll be shoveling driveways soon enough. No. I'll be shoveling driveways. You'll be calling the snow plow service."

Jamie hesitated, then tipped her glass toward me. "Okay," she smiled.

Though the Mathesons live only two houses away, the few hundred feet that separate us might as well be the Berlin wall. I live in a modest colonial with Rachel, my twelve-year-old daughter. The Mathesons live in a six-bedroom estate with a cedar shake roof and acres of woodland in back. Ted, an Internet security consultant, travels a lot. So does David, who lives in Philadelphia but spends most of his weekends out here in Chicago.

Jamie and I, both work-week widows, had gravitated toward each other, though in truth, I'm a little in awe of her. Not only is she president of the PTA, but she sings in the church choir, serves on the Village's quality of life committee, and used to be the soccer team parent. She's also a gourmet cook. We used to take brisk three-mile walks around the village, but after listening to her latest versions of crème brûlée or chicken in puff pastry with Boursin cheese, I'd be so ravenous afterwards that I'd eat everything in the fridge.

Tonight I didn't try to compete. Just steak, salad, and plenty of good wine. I was just opening up another bottle when David announced the meat was ready. I craned my neck. Black on the outside, pink in the middle. Perfect.

"Did 'ja see the new fence the Cavanaughs put up?" Ted said between bites a few minutes later. It was a warm autumn evening, and we were eating out on the deck. The sun had just dipped below the trees, and bursts of rosy light flickered across the yard.

"It looks nice," I ventured tentatively. Ted has his own take on things. I don't always agree with him.

"Are you kidding? It's an outrage." Ted sniffed. "They only did two sides. How cheap can you get?"

I swallowed. "Maybe that's all they could afford."

"I don't think so," Ted said in a singsong voice.

"Ted." Jamie's voice was sharp.

But the wine had evidently loosened Ted's tongue. "I happened to check their property tax bill a while back." His dark eyes glittered. "It's almost as high as ours." I almost asked how he'd managed to come across their property tax bills before I remembered they are public information. But even if they weren't, Ted would probably be able to get his hands on them. He was an expert on Internet security. I glanced at David, who dipped his head. We were thinking the same thing.

"People have different ways of doing things, honey," Jamie countered.

"Oh, Jamie, you're way too tolerant. You know—"

"More salad anyone?" I cut in, brandishing a pair of tongs.

Jamie shook her head, but I dished out more anyway. I turned an imploring face to David.

"Got a funny story to tell you," he started. I could have hugged him for coming to the rescue. "Well, not that funny. But interesting." He wiped his napkin across his mouth. "A client came to see me the other day." David trades foreign currency for a large Philadelphia bank. "Guy's expanding his business and was looking to hedge some German marks." Ted nodded. "Anyway, I'm sitting across the table from this guy, and something about him looks really familiar."

"What did he look like?" I asked.

"An average type. But it was driving me crazy. I was sure I knew this guy."

"Who was he?" Jamie gazed at David over the rim of her glass.

"I can't say. Client confidentiality. But for the purposes of tonight, let's call him 'Jack'".

Ted took a sip of wine.

"So. Jack keeps grinning, like he knows that I know him from someplace. Then, after we'd finished our business, he says, 'You're right, you know. You do know me from someplace.'"

Ted toyed with his fork.

David stroked his chin. "Turns out Jack was a Sixties radical. Part of a group called SHOUT."

"SHOUT?" I asked.

"Stop Human Oppression and Unrestrained Tyranny," David said.

Ted looked up. "Actually, it started out as the Society for Human Opportunity and Unlimited Trust."

"Interesting piece of trivia," I said. "How'd you know that?"

Ted shifted in his chair. "I don't know. I must have read it someplace."

David went on. "SHOUT had their own commune in West Philly, not far from the Penn campus. They were way out there, like SDS and the Weathermen. Made a lot of noise about cleansing the system and the people's revolution."

A hazy memory floated through time and connected in my brain. "Didn't they blow up a bank?"

"Two points." David raised his fingers. "They did, and a couple of people were killed."

Jamie frowned. "So how come this guy's out walking around free?"

"The prosecutors never proved he was part of the bombing. He claimed there was a 'gang of four'—two men and two women—who planned and executed the attack. Jack served a few years as an accessory. Everyone thought he was the bagman. But the ones who actually did the crime are still around—underground somewhere."

"Scumbags." Ted grumbled. A conservative Republican and Vietnam vet, Ted's idea of a hero is Oliver North. He even resembles the colonel, with a razor-edge haircut and deep-set eyes.

"Rizzo got even, though." David said.

"Who?" Jamie asked.

"Frank Rizzo, former mayor and police chief of Philadelphia. A few years after the bank, the Philadelphia police stormed SHOUT's commune and blew it up. Two SHOUT members were killed. The cops claimed SHOUT was armed to the teeth and was taking hostages."

"I remember," I said.

"Everybody knew it was a lie," David said. "It was payback for the bank. But the group fell apart after that."

"And this guy, your client – he was one of them?" I said.

"That's what he says," David said. "Once he was paroled, he stayed out of trouble." David spread his hands. "Remember, this was thirty years ago."

"Strange story." I poured the last of the wine into our glasses.

"Not that strange. The guy finally pulled his head out of his rear end," Ted said.

Wondering what Jamie thought, I stole a glance at her. Though she'd led a passionate fight against unnecessary development, helping to thwart a plan for a new village mall, she'd grown up in Connecticut on streets called "Elderberry" with lots of churches. She spent her life following the rules. Even now she was polite and gracious in her pearls, tailored slacks, and blond pageboy. It was Ted who stuck out his lower lip.

David rolled his wineglass between his palms. "So where were you during the sixties?" No one answered. "OK. I'll cop first. I dropped out of college and hitchhiked through Europe for a year."

"I didn't know that," I said.

He shrugged. "Not all that radical. But fun."

I cleared my throat, emboldened by his confession. "I lived in a commune and sold underground newspapers."

"You didn't!" Jamie's eyes grew wide.

I nodded, remembering how convinced I was that my life would never require a knowledge of furniture, china, or designer clothes. I was a crusader against a corrupt, repressive system. I wrote for the *Revolutionary Times* and read my "3M's": Mao, Marcuse, and Marx.

"What happened?" Jamie asked.

I shook my head. "It didn't last. They told me I was too bourgeoise. The most I could aspire to was running a safe-house."

"A wannabee, huh?" Ted sneered.

My spine stiffened. "What about you, Ted? Where were you during the revolution?"

He laughed. "ROTC then 'Nam. And damn proud of 'em both."

I suppressed an acid reply.

"Your turn, Jamie," David cut in.

"Well." She folded her hands in her lap. "I've never told anyone this." She looked at each of us.

I giggled. "Go ahead, Jamie. You're with friends."

She took a breath. "Okay. During our senior high school trip to Washington, we took a tour of the White House." She cast a sly look at us. "When we got to the Blue Room, I stuck a piece of gum behind the door, right on the door jamb."

I blinked. David stared. Ted snorted. "You what?"

She inspected her hands. "And you know what? When we went back a few years ago on one of those tours your Congressman sets up, I felt behind the door of the Blue Room. You're not going to believe it, but the gum was still there."

My mouth dropped open. No one said anything. I started to applaud. "You win, Jamie. You really stuck it to the system."

❖ ◆ ❖ ◆ ❖

Rachel and I stopped by Jamie's a couple of weeks later. Halloween was getting close, and Rachel wanted to be a hippie. I wondered if she and Conrad had overheard our stories the night they were over for dinner. Unless it was Conrad's idea. With his faded army jacket, pierced ear, and attitude, fourteen-year-old Conrad seemed like the antithesis of his parents.

I'd managed to scrounge a pair of old bell-bottoms and a peasant blouse from a trunk in the basement, but Rachel needed beads, sandals, and a peace symbol. I told her Jamie wouldn't have anything like that, but she insisted we try.

Jamie opened the door before we knocked. "Hi. I saw you on the street. Come on in."

She led us into the kitchen, a swirl of red quarry tile, gleaming white appliances, and lemon accents. I sat down at a glossy cedar table with a vase of mums on top. Doors and cabinets slid open. A minute later, two glasses of tea and a plate of homemade cookies appeared in front of us. The cookies were warm.

Between bites Rachel explained what she wanted. "I'm not sure I have anything," Jamie frowned, "but why don't we take a look. Come on. I'll show you." She waved at me. "We'll be right back, Ellie."

"Is Conrad here?" Rachel asked as they climbed the stairs.

"No, he's at—" Jamie's voice faded away, and I couldn't make out where Conrad was supposed to be.

I munched cookies, idly scanning some papers on the kitchen table. Minutes from the Quality of Life meeting. The agenda centered on whether to fund a proposed historical society with village money. And how to organize next year's Fourth of July celebration.

The trill of the phone broke my concentration. Should I answer it? The phone was mounted on the wall near the refrigerator. It rang again. Maybe Jamie couldn't hear it upstairs. I stood up. No. This wasn't my house. I rocked back and forth. It's hard for me to leave a ringing phone unanswered. After the fourth ring, Ted's voice boomed out. "This is 555-9876. Leave a message." That was Ted. Nothing cute. Barely polite.

A man's voice followed. "It's been a long time, friend." I stared at the phone. "We're anxious to talk and smell the jasmine. We have a lot of catching up to do. We'll expect to hear from you soon." The caller disconnected with a click. An uneasy feeling skittered around inside of me. Talk and smell the jasmine?

A few minutes later, Rachel came down, happily clutching a string of blue beads. Jamie was behind her.

"Let's see them." I inspected them carefully. "These are too good," I said to Jamie.

"Mom!" Rachel cried in dismay.

"What are they?"

Jamie shrugged. "I don't know. Lapis lazuli maybe."

Rachel's eyes were shooting darts at me, but I shook my head. "I can't let you do this, Jamie. What if something happens to them?"

Rachel whined. "But I'll be careful."

I raised an eyebrow. "Like you were with my bracelet?" Rachel had lost my favorite a few months ago, a sterling band shot through with filigree.

"Oh, come on Ellie," Jamie said. "I trust her."

I looked at Jamie, then Rachel. They stood next to each other in solidarity, Jamie smiling, Rachel's face a mix of anxiety and determination. I relented. "I don't have a chance against both of you."

Rachel threw her arms around me.

I hugged her back. "By the way, Jamie, someone left you a strange message. Something about talking and smelling the jasmine."

She walked over to the machine and replayed the tape. Her face was blank. "It must be a wrong number. I'll erase it." She started to hit a button on the machine.

"But what if it's for Ted?"

"Unlikely," she said testily. "He talks to everyone on his cell phone."

"But if you don't know who it is, shouldn't you save it for him?"

Reluctantly she took her finger off the button. "You're probably right."

Just then Conrad pushed through the door. When he saw Rachel, he brushed by her with a lazy smile. Rachel's face grew crimson, and she seemed to forget how to move her arms and legs. Conrad didn't look at all awkward, his eyes passing over her as if he expected nothing less than adoration. I bit the inside of my cheek.

❖ ◆ ❖ ◆ ❖

David and I pulled into the driveway after dinner Saturday night. Warm and languid from too much food and wine, we were discussing whether Danny DeVito or Joe Pesci made the better anti-hero. I liked Danny DeVito because he was funny, shrewd, and his wife was a riot on "Cheers". David liked Joe Pesci. More versatile, he could do drama and slapstick, sometimes in the same film.

"Unfair," I said. "What about 'War of the Roses'? DeVito played it straight."

"But he wasn't the hero," David said. "Or the anti-hero. He was the narrator. The Greek chorus."

"Oh, and Pesci was heroic in all those 'Home Alone' disasters?"

"He sang in one of his films, but I forget which."

"Joe Pesci sang?" I giggled. "Okay. That'll get you two points."

He gently cuffed my shoulder. "You're a tough sell, lady."

I unlocked the garage door. Inside an unnatural stillness greeted us, as if someone had abruptly stopped talking but a faint echo still hung in the air. Upstairs blue light from the TV spilled into the hall. The springs of the couch squeaked, and I heard rustles and a grunt. I climbed the steps and peered into the family room.

Conrad was on one end of the couch, Rachel on the other. Their faces were flushed, and the air felt steamy. The television threw spiked shadows on the floor. Rachel tried to flash me a guileless smile. I stomped to the coffee table, littered with a videocassette sleeve, the remote, and a couple of glasses. My breath was shallow. Rachel was only twelve years old, damn it.

"Do your parents know you're here, Conrad?"

He shrugged, seemingly fascinated by something on the wall. I picked up the phone. By the time I'd punched in four of the seven digits, he apparently had a change of heart. "My mother's out of town, Mrs. Foreman. At my grand mom's. I don't know where my father is."

He was pleading. I hesitated, looked back at him, then punched in the last few numbers. This was my daughter. He shrank back on the couch.

Ted picked up right away. "Hi, Ted. This is Ellie." I explained the situation as dispassionately as I could. He stormed in minutes later and dragged Conrad out. We heard him through the closed door. "You idiot. You know the rules. What the hell were you thinking?"

I told Rachel we'd talk about it in the morning. I needed time to figure out what to say. She slunk off to bed. David helped me straighten up.

"It's probably my fault," I said, plumping the cushions on the couch.

"How can you say that?" he said.

"She sees us. We're not married."

"Ellie. We're adults. She's not."

I sighed. "She thinks she is."

"Oh come on. Every kid experiments with sex."

"David. She's only twelve. Conrad's fourteen. Two years makes a big difference."

"And you're the one who lived in a commune." He smiled. "Don't tell me you never played Spin the Bottle."

"Rachel and Conrad weren't playing Spin the Bottle." I took the glasses into the kitchen. "Rachel might as well have been Lindsay Dellinger."

David followed me in. "Who?"

"Lindsay Dellinger. She was one of *those* girls." I rinsed the glasses in the sink. "You remember, don't you?" He offered me a slow smile. "See?" I waggled an angry finger.

"I don't know Lindsay Dellinger."

"Doesn't matter. Here it is almost forty years later and the only thing I remember about the woman is her reputation. Which, when I describe it to you, immediately prompts you to leer. What if Rachel ends up like her?"

I bent down and sprinkled soap in the dishwasher, expecting one of David's calm, rational replies that would reveal the flaws in my logic. That would convince me Rachel was in no danger of being permanently branded. It didn't come. I straightened up. He was looking past me. "David?"

"Sorry. I was just thinking."

"What?"

"Remember the guy I told you about the night Ted and Jamie were over for dinner?"

"Jack, the radical who wanted to expand his business?"

"Yeah. Well, he backed out of the deal. He decided he didn't want to be global after all."

"Really." I wiped my hands on a towel.

He nodded. "What you said about reputations reminded me."

We started back towards the family room. "You're not surprised, are you?" He shrugged. "People can't paper over their pasts with dollar bills. Or marks. It's part of their history."

David sat on the couch. "But he'd come so far. Remade his life. Why would he throw away an opportunity to take it to the next level?"

I dropped down next to him. "Maybe he wasn't sure he wanted it anymore. Maybe he couldn't reconcile the image of what he was becoming with what he used to be."

"Does that mean he deserves to live an unfulfilled life?"

"No. It's just that some people never escape their past."

"You did."

"I was only a wannabee, remember? And in my own way, I paid a price."

David draped his arm around my shoulder. "But what you did wasn't intrinsically wrong. You were following through on something you believed in. Why should you have to pay a price?"

I leaned against him. "Oh, David, you're so noble. You still believe that people act out of principle, not self-interest."

"Is that what Jack did?"

"I have no idea." I settled his hand in the crook of my neck. "I guess I'm just jealous."

"Of what?"

"Your moral certainty. I wish I was as sure as you." I kissed his fingers.

"Don't be. I didn't expect Jack to pull out. We'd just talked a week before."

"Oh?"

"We were going over some hedging procedures on the phone. When we were done, I asked him whether the acronym for SHOUT had changed at some point. You remember what Ted said at dinner."

"Right."

"Well, Jack was so quiet I thought we'd been disconnected. Then he asked me how I knew about that."

"What'd you say?"

David shrugged. "That my girlfriend's neighbor had read it in the paper."

❖ ◆ ❖ ◆ ❖

The next morning I told Rachel she was too young for the kind of behavior I'd seen last night and that I didn't want her seeing Conrad alone any more. She barely spoke to me afterwards. I counted up the days until she turned twenty. Only eight more years.

I debated whether I should say anything to Jamie. Ted had probably filled her in, and I didn't want her to think I'd gone ballistic. But I didn't want her to think it had gone unnoticed, either. As it happened, the only time I saw her was in passing, and she was preoccupied. Her mother had suddenly suffered a stroke. She was going back to Connecticut to settle her into a nursing home.

When I was young Halloween used to be my favorite holiday. Now though, horror has gone mainstream, and it's become distasteful. Even so, I stayed home to "ooo" and "ah" over the headless monsters, blood-soaked vampires, and fearsome witches roaming the neighborhood. Rachel baby-sits for a lot of them, and I felt obligated to help grease the wheels of her burgeoning enterprise. What they call in marketing "extending good-will".

Between doling out plenty of candy and appropriating more for ourselves, we tried to watch a movie, but we were barely past the credits when a thump sounded at the door. Thinking it must be kids, I asked Rachel to open it. When I heard her scream, I bolted from the couch.

Rachel was in the hall whimpering, one hand clasped across her mouth. The door was closed but not latched. I opened it and peered out. A dead raccoon lay sprawled on the mat. Some of its ribs protruded through its torso, and pieces of bloody entrails with bits of shiny white gristle gleamed in the porch light. Roadkill. I gagged and slammed the door.

❖ ◆ ❖ ◆ ❖

David, jetlagged from a trip to Zurich, didn't come out that weekend. It was just as well. Since the raccoon incident Rachel seemed to regress, content to stay home with me. After a movie, in which Danny DeVito effectively reinforced his anti-hero status, at least to me, I flipped on CNN.

The anchor announced that a former Sixties radical had been killed in a suspicious fire out East. Jack Halsey, according to the newscaster, was once associated with SHOUT, a Philadelphia group responsible for blowing up a bank thirty years ago. Arson was suspected in Halsey's death. I called David. He was grim. Jack Halsey had been his client.

The explosion woke me from a dead sleep. Glass shattered. Alarms blared. Adrenaline coursed through every pore. I tore out of bed, screaming at Rachel to wake up. A pungent smell wafted through the air, and it was chilly inside. I understood why when, instead of windows, I saw gaping holes framed with shards of glass. We stumbled down the stairs and raced out of the house.

Though the smell was stronger outside, my house, except for the black spaces where my windows used to be, was intact. But alarms still pierced the air. I ran toward the sounds. They stopped at the Mathesons'.

The blast had thrown most of the house up in the air, snapping walls and furniture into giant pick-up sticks. The walls at the front of the house had collapsed, leaving a mass of fiery debris. A cloud of dust hovered above, a pale fog against the dark sky.

As I drew closer, alarms were replaced by other sounds of disaster. Sirens cut through the air. Neighbors shouted. Doors slammed. Police and firemen converged on the scene. Hoses were uncoiled and jets of water flooded the house. More people arrived, including the fire marshal with his dog. He promptly walked the German shepherd around the perimeter of the property. The dog kept his head down, snuffling everything in its path. That's how they found Jamie, dirty and muddy, in the woods behind the house. Dazed and in shock, her leg was broken. The EMTs took her to the hospital.

I didn't get much sleep that night. Neither, apparently, did village detective Mike O'Malley. He was at my door by eight the next morning, with Special Agent Reese Brightman. I had met O'Malley, a tall, freckled, no-nonsense cop, the previous summer, and he raised an eyebrow in recognition. Brightman was short and wiry, and despite the blustery morning, wore sunglasses.

"Detective O'Malley." I greeted him. "I didn't think we'd meet again this soon."

"Ms. Foreman," O'Malley said, stepping inside into the hall. "I hear you know the Matheson family."

I nodded. "What about Conrad and Ted? Have you found them?"

"We found the kid. He was spending the night at a friend's," O'Malley said.

"Thank god."

"But we haven't located the husband. You have any idea where he might be?"

I shook my head. "He traveled a lot."

O'Malley shifted his weight. "Tell me, Ms. Foreman," he said, "did the Mathesons have a strong marriage?"

I twisted one hand in the other. "It had its ups and downs."

"Any infidelity? Affairs?"

"Not that I know of." I scanned both their faces. "Why?"

O'Malley and Brightman exchanged glances. The FBI agent nodded. "We found a body in the house," O'Malley said. "Pretty well charred. A female." I swallowed. "She was killed before the bomb went off." My hand flew to my throat. "With a kitchen knife."

"And you think—"

Brightman cut me off. "We don't know what we think. What about Mrs. Matheson? Wasn't she supposed to be out of town?"

An edgy feeling started to spread through my gut. "She was in Connecticut for a few days, taking care of her mother."

"What do you know about Mrs. Matheson's past?" Agent Brightman interrupted.

"Her past?"

"Was she involved in any political activities as a young woman?"

"Jamie?" I said. "She's about as political as Martha Stewart."

Brightman's mouth tightened.

The news reported that the victim inside the Matheson house was Pamela Winger, a former radical implicated in a Philadelphia bank explosion that killed two people thirty years ago. She'd been missing, but according to a source, she and Jack Halsey had stayed in touch. Winger apparently suspected that Jamie killed Halsey and flew out to confront her. The source, who had to be Brightman, theorized that Jamie killed Winger too, then planted the bomb to destroy the evidence.

They took Jamie to the Metropolitan Correctional Center and charged her with arson and first-degree murder. A few days later I got a message she wanted to see me. I almost didn't go, but they said I was the only person besides Conrad she'd written down on her visitor request form.

I drove downtown to the MCC, showed my ID, and was escorted to a room with several tables. I slid into an empty chair. Twenty minutes later, Jamie hobbled in on crutches. Purple smudges ringed her eyes, and her hair was dirty and matted. The prison uniform, an orange jump suit, hung on her slender frame, but she maneuvered the crutches gracefully and sat down as if we were at the Ritz Carlton for tea.

"How's Conrad?"

"He's fine," I said. "He's at the Whitmans'. Sally said he could stay as long as he wanted."

"Her face relaxed. "She's a friend, Ellie. So are you."

I felt my stomach twist. "That makes one of us." She reeled back as if I'd slapped her. "How could you deceive me like this?" She gave me a blank look. "PTA, church choir, soccer mom. The gum story really had me going."

"Ellie, you don't understand."

"What's there to understand? You were one of the SHOUT people who blew up that bank, and you've been living a nice white-bread life for yourself ever since." I shook my head. "And I thought you wouldn't step on a crack in the sidewalk."

"Ellie, you're wrong."

"I guess so." I leaned forward. "You knew who 'Jack' was the minute David first talked about him at our house, didn't you? Then, when you got that cryptic phone message about jasmine, you realized Jack had tracked you down. So you went to Philadelphia to make sure he wouldn't expose you. The trips to your mother's were a lie."

She repeated herself. "You don't understand."

"But Jack didn't cooperate, did he? He'd already taken the heat for you once. So when he threatened to turn you in, you killed him. Pamela Winger too." Jamie squirmed in her seat. "Where did you learn how to handle explosives, Jamie? Did SHOUT teach you? Or did you teach them?"

Jamie raised her hands, as if warding me off.

"What I don't understand is why you came back. After you killed Jack, why didn't you disappear like you did thirty years ago?"

She blinked. "Ellie, go away. This visit is over."

"I know. It was motherly love. You just had to see Conrad."

She pressed her palms together so hard that her nails whitened. "Ted called me at my mother's. He said Conrad was sick and I had to come home. I caught the first flight back. When I walked in, the body of that— that woman was on the kitchen floor. I panicked. I was running out of the house to get help when the bomb exploded."

I stared at her for a minute, then stood up. "Nice try, Jamie. Or whoever you are." I pushed the chair back and left.

I waited for Ted to surface, but after a month I realized he never would. I was surfing the net one night, and just for fun, I ran a search on SHOUT. The results produced several items, including an article from *Philadelphia* magazine that traced the group's history. I read it carefully, but it never mentioned the group changing its name. But Ted had said he'd read about it. The night he and Jamie were over for dinner. I checked again.

That's when I knew.

Ted. Always on the move. The Ollie North persona. It was the perfect cover. It was Ted who went to Philadelphia. Ted who killed Halsey and Pamela Winger. Ted who lured Jamie home, intending to destroy her too.

I called Brightman the next morning, but he was skeptical. Ever since Kathleen Soliah was arrested, the Bureau's been anxious to close the book on the Sixties, and he persisted in his theory that Jamie was part of SHOUT. But David found her a good lawyer, and she made bail. According to her lawyer, she has a good chance.

We never did find out why Jack Halsey backed out of the currency deal with David. Maybe, after he tracked down Ted, he wanted to keep his money liquid. Maybe he thought he'd need it to "manage" Ted. Or maybe he decided he didn't want to be a capitalist after all.

I was shoveling the walk that winter when Conrad showed up. The mound of debris that used to be the Matheson's house was now covered with pristine snow; the rumors were that someone had bought the lot and would rebuild in the spring. Jamie and Conrad were renting a few blocks away, but I hadn't seen much of her. She'd quit the PTA, didn't go to church; she was keeping a low profile. Conrad studied the property then strolled over to my house. He raised an arm in greeting.

I leaned on the shovel. "How are you, Conrad?"

"Okay." He was carrying an olive green bundle under his arm.

"I'm glad." My anger at his behavior had long ago faded. He had his own problems; he'd carry his father's burden forever.

"I— I came by to apologize for something," he said. "Last Halloween. The raccoon on your porch? It was me. I was mad. I hope you forgive me."

I looked at him. The earring was gone, and he'd cut his hair. "It's forgotten," I said. "Another life. But thank you for being honest about it."

He nodded again. "I'd like to give this—or have you give this—to Rachel." He handed me the green bundle.

I shook it out. It was his army jacket. I smiled.

"It's the real thing. My mother got it at an Army-Navy surplus store in Philadelphia."

I corrected him. "You mean your father."

He shook his head. "No." He took the jacket back. "It was my mom's." He held it up. I squinted at it. Just above the breast pocket was a tiny embroidered white flower.

"It's supposed to be jasmine," he said. "I thought Rachel would like it." He handed it back to me and started to walk away.

I stared after him. Jasmine. Talk and smell the jasmine. Jamie was Jasmine. Jamie and Ted were in SHOUT together. I clutched the jacket to my chest. I had been wrong. Ted didn't blow up his own house, abandon his family, vanish without a trace. It was Jamie. Tired of the lies and subterfuge over thirty years, she must have decided to take matters into her own hands. My eyes drifted to the woods at the back of the lot where they found her; dirty, muddy, her leg broken. Ted had never been found. Could there be other charred remains—besides Pamela Winger's—somewhere on the property?

"Conrad?"

He turned around and gazed at me, his shoulders hunched.

"Why are you giving this away?"

"I'm getting rid of some stuff. We're moving."

"Moving?"

"As soon as my mom comes back for me."

"Your mother's gone?"

He stiffened. "It's only been a few days. She'll be back. She said so."

My breath caught in my throat. I pursed my lips. He turned away. I watched him trudge through the snow, fourteen but already stooped like an old man.

Libby Fischer Hellmann, an award-winning Chicago crime thriller author, has published eight novels. Her ninth thriller, A BITTER VEIL, *is set in revolutionary Iran, and is slated for release in March, 2012.* SET THE NIGHT ON FIRE *(2010), is a stand-alone thriller that goes back, in part, to the late Sixties in Chicago. She also writes two crime fiction series. The first features Chicago PI Georgia Davis and includes the hard-boiled* EASY INNOCENCE *(2008) and* DOUBLEBACK *(2009). In addition, there are four novels in the Ellie Foreman series, which Libby describes as a cross between "Desperate Housewives" and "24." Libby has also published over 15 short stories in* NICE GIRL DOES NOIR *and has edited the acclaimed crime fiction anthology,* CHICAGO BLUES. *She has been nominated twice for the Anthony Award, and once for the Agatha. All her work is available digitally. Originally from Washington DC, she has lived in Chicago for 30 years and claims they'll take her out of there feet first.*

Learn more at her website:

www.libbyhellmann.com

A BRIEF FORAY OUT OF CRIME FICTION... AND INTO OTHER WORLDS

The following piece was written for a collection of essays called *Mystery Muses*, in which 100 mystery writers were asked to write about a book that had influenced their own work. Figuring that people were going to gravitate toward Christie and Poe, I ransacked my memory for something a little different and I came up with Asimov's famous science fiction mystery, *The Caves of Steel*.

I often think that I might have a science fiction mystery of my own in me, waiting to be written. I cut my teeth on science fiction, reading it throughout my formative years and writing it during my formative years as a writer. In fact, I have read and written in many genres over the years—mystery, science fiction, mainstream, fantasy, literary, young adult. I love writing mysteries, but I am a mystery writer by profession solely because *Artifacts* was the first fiction I sold. If my first sale had been a science fiction short story, I might well be doing something else. Life takes its little twists and turns, and sometimes it is good to look back and ask oneself, "How did I get here, anyway?"

I continue to read widely. I have a historical novel in my head, begging to come out and play. One day soon, I shall write it. One of the blessings of this new electronic world is that I can write anything I please, without worrying that bookstores won't know where to put my books on the shelves. My only concern is that my readers be able to find me.

In celebration of this freedom to write whatever story my muse is whispering in my ear, I'm including two non-mystery pieces in this collection—this *Mystery Muses* essay on *The Caves of Steel* and a previously unpublished science fiction short story called *Jesup's Flight.* I hope those of you who aren't ordinarily science fiction readers will bear with me. This story, written years before my first Faye Longchamp archaeological mystery, looks at some of the same issues I address when writing about Faye, a biracial woman living in the South who is deeply knowledgeable about the history of the region. In my Faye Longchamp mysteries, I can show the faces of people who were im-prisoned in our country until the mid-nineteenth century by the institution of slavery.

In *Jesup's Flight,* I can take a look at the same issue from a very different angle, because when I'm writing speculative fiction, I can manipulate history and even the laws of nature. Perhaps this little secret will help people who are not science fiction fans will understand those of us who are:

The technology is not the point.

If it helps you enjoy the story, you can skip over my explanation of the (heavily fictionalized) science behind Jesup's flight suit and imagine that I typed "Blah, blah, blah, blah, blah." This story, like any good story, is not about gadgets. It is about the way the primary character is affected by the events around him and by the world he lives in. This story is different from my mysteries only in the fact that Jesup doesn't live in the same world that you and I do. In the end, this doesn't matter. We feel for him because he is a human being, no matter where he lives.

Jesup's world is a place where the Civil War never happened and where slavery survived into the early 21st century. It will not survive much longer, even in that world, for purely economic reasons. It is much cheaper to pay people minimum wage and send them home to fend for themselves on those paltry wages than it is to provide them food and shelter and medical care. In this world—and perhaps this would be true in ours—slavery is only cost-effective for people so highly talented that they would be very expensive to hire if they were free. They are such valuable individuals that their owners can even afford to give them a lavish lifestyle and attend to their every desire...except freedom.

In this world, everybody wants to own an MBA.

But what does this strange kind of enslavement do to a brilliant and sensitive man...a man like the title character, Jesup? Well, eventually, Jesup learns to fly...

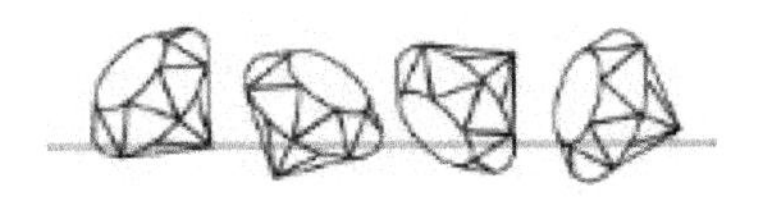

YES, IT CAN BE DONE:
The Caves of Steel
by Isaac Asimov

YES, IT CAN BE DONE:
The Caves of Steel by Isaac Asimov

An essay on the relationship between science fiction and crime fiction

Some people don't respond well to being told, "It can't be done." The seminal science fiction editor John W. Campbell once said it was impossible to write a book that was both a good mystery and a good science fiction novel. He explained that, at the climactic moment, the detective could produce some bit of technology that would solve his problems for him. In other words, books set in the future couldn't possibly play fair with the reader.

In Isaac Asimov's autobiography, *I. Asimov*, he said he "privately thought that this was a foolish statement, because it was only necessary to set the background at the start and avoid introducing anything new in the remainder of the book. You would then have a science fiction story that was legitimate."

In *The Caves of Steel*, the good doctor wrote that legitimate science fiction mystery story. The mystery is as finely crafted and as fully realized as its futuristic setting. Reading *The Caves of Steel* is like gazing through a telescope fitted with expertly ground lenses. Look through one end, and you learn something about the world around you. Turn the scope around and look through the other lens, and the world looks different. (Actually it looks very, very small.) Everything you see is still true, but your perception has changed. A good mystery can change your world view. So can good science fiction. This book is both.

Asimov sets the rules of his future Earth early, and his characters—a human detective and his robotic partner—live by them. Even better, those rules drive the plot. When the detective makes a deduction that proves wrong, it's not because the robot's behavior is inconsistent or unpredictable. It's simply because the detective doesn't understand it.

Most satisfying of all, the ticking-clock ending neatly avoids the contrived feeling we've all gotten from less-successful stories. That clock is ticking because his partner, the robot, is who he is. His cooperation will end at midnight, for perfectly logical reasons, and our hero must set the world right before that happens.

That hero, Lije Bailey, is a classic mystery protagonist—a good cop, a family man, but a loner at heart. Solving this crime isn't just a job to him, because he values justice. He's a successful character, but we've met others like him. Before this book was published in 1954, nobody had ever met anyone like his partner, R. Daneel Olivaw, a machine who looks like a human being and whose newly programmed appetite for justice makes him act an awful lot like one. Dr. Asimov said that Daneel may be his most popular character. I know he's my favorite.

Dr. Asimov was one of us, a lifelong mystery reader. Actually, he was a lifelong omnivorous reader. His descriptions of the magical library of his youth take me back to the bookmobile that I ransacked weekly as a child. I remember exactly where my favorite books were shelved—Nancy Drew's adventures, Alfred Hitchcock's anthologies, and the long row of Robert Heinlein's juvenile novels. (Imagine my chagrin when I learned that Mr. Heinlein referred to his juveniles as "boys' books." Trust me, I was never a boy.)

When I hear the word "library," I feel an air conditioner blast out air with that peculiar bookmobile smell. (I think it was the ink for the machine that stamped the due date in each book.) When I see my own books in libraries, the book-loving child in me gets a shivery thrill.

Like Dr. Asimov, my path took me from the library to a science education. Also like him, I eventually left the science I loved for the literature I love even more. My mysteries don't incorporate science fiction (yet), but the science is there. A writer can't help putting herself into her work. Constructed my mysteries have required me to bone up on meteorology, geology, archaeology, physics...

And I love it.

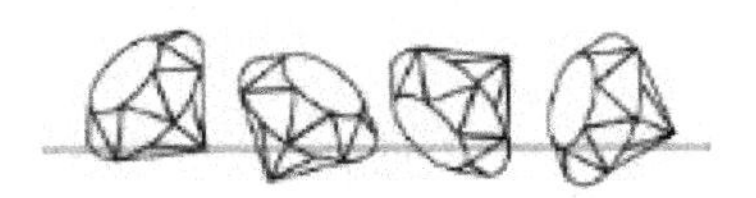

JESUP'S FLIGHT

JESUP'S FLIGHT

If Jesup's master had not left the Flightsuit® in plain sight, the unfortunate incident could have been averted. But how was Nathan to suspect that Jesup was capable of such a thing? Perhaps he should have known something was amiss when Jesup began calling him "Master Nate" again.

Nathan had laughed at first, saying, "Jesup, you sound appallingly twentieth-century."

"Yes, Master Nate, I do," replied the older man, who met his eyes firmly in a manner Nathan's father would never have permitted and glanced at the slaves' rings he had worn embedded in his index fingers since birth.

Nathan had pleaded with his friend, but Jesup stubbornly clung to the ridiculous title. Nathan had been three feet tall when he first instructed Jesup never to use the term "Master" again. Nathan had lost that battle, of course. Nathan's father always required Jesup to show adequate respect, and Jesup never once wavered in using the prescribed honorific while Walton Parker was alive, even when toweling the boy off after his nightly bath.

Whether or not Nathan liked to think of Jesup as a slave, the facts were simple. Nathan's father had held title to Jesup's parents, free and clear. Therefore, he had owned Jesup since the moment of his birth, and maybe before. The Supreme Court had yet to rule on that point.

Jesup's original intention had not been to run away. It most certainly had not been to steal the Flightsuit®. He had merely intended to read the instructions on the Flightsuit®.

His science education had not progressed beyond university physics and he could not fathom how the thing could possibly work. It was apparently a skintight elastic jumpsuit, but Jesup was fairly certain that the suit served only as support for a grid of molecular circuitry in the shape of the wearer's body. He consulted the instruction booklet, but was disappointed to find that it was written for a reader with even less technical sophistication than Jesup possessed.

> *Every schoolchild learns about molecular motion,* the brochure began, *and every schoolchild learns the classic illustration of the desk and the wall. The teacher points out that every molecule in every desk beneath every student is moving randomly all the time. If even a small fraction of these molecules moved non-randomly in the same direction, the desk (and the student in it) would slam into the classroom wall. The scientists who developed the Flightsuit® have developed a means to affect air molecules around a human body in just such a way.*

Jesup laid the instructions down and stripped naked. As he tugged the suit onto his body, he wondered how he would explain this to Nathan if he got caught. He snugged his feet into the built-in boots and tugged hard at the body of the suit. Nathan was shorter than Jesup but he was heavier, so Jesup was able to work the suit around his body. He pulled the right sleeve on and thrust his left arm into its sleeve, too, tugging hard on the attached glove. The suit was sturdy, but it had been custom-made for Nathan. Jesup's larger frame was outside its design limits. The left glove tore across the back of his hand and, relieved of its tension, crept up until its useless fingers dangled from Jesup's wrist.

Now there was a real need to explain his behavior to his master. Jesup decided to think about this later. He pulled up the suit's hood and continued studying the suit's instructions.

> *The Flightsuit® encourages air molecules above and below the body to move slightly upward, creating lift. Similarly, the Suit's gloves repel air molecules and its boots attract them, creating a push to drive the wearer forward.*
>
> *Speed is controlled by varying the glove area exposed to oncoming air. Extend both hands, fingers spread, for top speed. Hold a hand to the chest for deceleration. To land, assume a standing position, hands and feet pointing downward. The position analyzer optimizes the vector sum of the forces downward from the gloves, upward from the boots, and downward from gravity, allowing a soft landing every time.*
>
> *The position analyzer is a formidable safety feature. Should the wearer accidentally assume a head-down position, the suit will exert a repulsive force downward sufficient to support the body. Landing cannot be accomplished from any position other than the standing position described above.*

The brochure certainly made flying sound easy enough. Jesup walked into the back lawn of his master's estate, swung his right arm upward, and lifted easily from the ground. The suit really did make flying easy, like bobbing atop ocean swells.

When Jesup saw that the contraption really did what it was supposed to do, his mind settled into the familiar groove of assessing profit potential. This technology had widespread implications—for mass transit, for manufacture and transport of delicate items. Hell, there was a fortune to be made just in franchising to amusement parks.

He rolled onto his back to think, and the suit adjusted to his new position, probably thanks to its "position analyzer," whatever the hell that was. Why was all this potential being wasted on a rich man's toy?

Perhaps the manufacturers of the Flightsuit® had been long on ideas and short on cash. Perhaps they had manufactured a few suits and sold them to corporate giants, the very individuals who would have capital available for investment. His master could certainly be counted among the corporate elite.

Jesup had run Parker Petroleum for twenty-seven years now, first for Nathan's father and now for Nathan himself. Jesup knew that he had earned back the value of his parents' purchase price, his clothing, his food, his housing, his medical care, and his Ivy League education, many times over. He knew more about Nathan's business than Nathan knew himself. Therefore, he knew exactly how much expendable income Nathan had, and he knew that it was more than sufficient to provide startup capital for Flightsuit®. Jesup was fairly certain that he could talk Nathan into investing. He was absolutely certain that the investment would be profitable.

Jesup rolled over, planning to land and get to work on the Flightsuit® deal. He found himself floating higher than he had thought. He scanned the unfamiliar streets below, assumed the landing position, and began dropping slowly to search for landmarks.

A small craft passed above him, lowering its landing gear. He was in no immediate danger, but the vessel was closer than he would have liked. He checked its flight direction and felt his stomach lurch. He was a quarter-mile from the New Orleans International Airport and, while he was still too low to be much of a threat to air traffic, it was a solid bet that the air traffic controllers knew he was there. This did not strike Jesup as a good thing.

On cue, he heard a distant siren. He thrust his arms forward to fly away and found his progress impeded by the torn glove. This problem effectively halved his forward thrust. He dangled his left hand downward to reduce the drag. It hung blackly from the sleeve of the white Flightsuit® and its slaves' ring glinted in the sun. A passer-by looked up and saw Jesup, his ring brazenly on display.

"Runaway slave!" the woman screamed, and Jesup's fate was sealed.

He should have flown home. Nathan would have known he wasn't a runaway and the whole thing would have been declared a misunderstanding. He should have flown home, but even a mind like Jesup's can be clouded by panic, and he had never in his life been in physical danger. He flew over the levee and bolted upriver as fast as the suit would fly.

The wet wind on his face cleared his mind a bit and he began to consider the best ways to escape detection. The woman had seen a runaway slave, but she had no way to know his identity. That made remote tracking by GPS difficult at best, until and unless Nathan reported him missing. Of course, few individuals were jetting along at a hundred feet above land surface, so his first action should be to get low.

He pointed his right hand downward, keeping the useless left glove clasped to his chest. Riding just above the dark water, he knew that GPSTrak's slave locating system would never be able to distinguish him from an individual in a fast boat.

Very good, he told himself. *Now, where in hell are you going?*

When he saw the rusted distillation towers rising above the levee and flew by the abandoned shipping terminals of the old oil refineries, he knew exactly where he was going. A few minutes passed and he lifted himself over the levee and headed for the abandoned road to the old Parker plantation. He flew to it as surely as if he had never left it, with the confidence of a man who knew that it belonged to him more than to any other human alive.

He had been there once before when Nathan was a child and Jesup's sole assignment had been to care for him. GPSTrak was new in those days, and unaccompanied travel outside the secured cars of the slave transit system was still new to Jesup—and new to Nathan, too, because the boy and his father's slave went everywhere together. Jesup had been granted the use of Mr. Parker's antique pickup truck for the day, and he had been nearly as excited as the boy.

They had bumped down the old River Road, past broken remnants of the great sugar plantations and the rusting hulks of the oil refineries that had temporarily replaced them. Jesup turned down an unpaved road that passed beside one of these refineries and tunneled deep into the subtropical underbrush. By this time, Nathan was bouncing against the safety belt and demanding, "Are we there yet? Are we there yet?"

Nathan was out of the pickup before the ignition was off, yelling "What is this place?" as a darkened building loomed over them.

"Your grandfather's grandfather's grandfather's grandfather's grandfather's grandfather had it built in 1830. It was his home," Jesup said, unloading the picnic basket.

"It belongs to Daddy? I'm going in there!" The little boy hurtled through the overgrown gardens where the old house waited. Jesup rushed after him, lest the structure finally lose its integrity and rain two-hundred-year-old bricks and timbers on the child's head.

The old plantation house was actually fairly sound. Years before, Nathan's father had hired historical architects to stabilize it. The cost of a full restoration exceeded even Mr. Parker's considerable family pride, so the structure stood interrupted in the act of falling down, a relic whose appointment with entropy had been temporarily postponed.

Jesup led Nathan through his ancestral home, testing the floor in each room before allowing the boy to enter. Because the house had been occupied for a century before the family abandoned it for the more modern mansion they currently occupied, the interior reflected the tastes of five generations of Parkers.

Flocked Victorian wallpapers peeled from walls crowned with Greek Revival plaster work. The symmetrical floor plan had been marred by the addition of a small bathroom. Someone had clumsily wired the gas jets for electricity. Jesup caressed the smooth lines of an Art Deco wall sconce and made a mental note to tell his master that the house was not yet stripped quite bare of its treasures.

Jesup could tell that Nathan burned to rush up the spiral staircase. Unsure of its condition, he lifted the boy in his arms, hauled him bodily outside, and ordered him to play.

Jesup was pouring the lemonade when Nathan screamed. Six years as a nursemaid had given Jesup a mother's discriminating ear. This scream was real.

He stumbled to his feet, looking for the boy, but he was alone in the middle of a garden slowly returning to the Louisiana swamp.

Jesup ran, calling the boy, thinking that the phone in his pocket could locate him in a heartbeat. GPSTrak continuously monitored the whereabouts of everyone in the world—except, of course, for free adults who didn't want to be found.

He could have patched into the system within moments, but he hesitated. GPSTrak was for finding criminals and runaway slaves and dead bodies, not for finding little boys who couldn't—mustn't—have wandered too far. GPSTrak was for finding children who had drowned in the swamp. GPSTrak was for finding children whose bodies were swelling as the rattlesnake venom began its work. GPSTrak was for—

"Jesup."

The little voice was faint, but Jesup followed it to the rear of the house, hurdling the low brick wall that obscured Nathan from view.

"Yes, Master Nathan."

The response was weak but definite. "Stop calling me Master."

Jesup cradled the bloodied head and mashed the gaping wound shut with his shirttail. Nathan had come upon the foundation of the old plantation kitchen. Any redblooded child confronted with a low, narrow wall will climb onto it and walk it like a tightrope. Any parent knows this.

And any former child can also tell you that sometimes you fall off. And sometimes you land on things you wish you hadn't. Like bricks. Pointed shards of broken bricks.

With his free hand, Jesup reached for his phone and activated the GPSTrak emergency band. Let the paramedics curse him for calling them out for a playground injury. His master had the means to foot the bill. Maybe if they arrived quickly and applied the dermatologic adhesive properly, maybe then his Nathan wouldn't carry a scar from this day.

Jesup sang tunelessly to the dazed child while they waited for the chopper. He looked at the bloodied brick at his feet and considered the possibility that one of his great-great-great-great-great-great-great-great grandfathers had crafted it with his own hands. His eyes raked across the fields where his ancestors might have planted and hoed and reaped. All traces of their homes had collapsed and rotted away. As he sat there, he truly believed that he never wanted to see this place again.

Yet he had returned. And he was kneeling by the crumbling foundation of the old kitchen, swathed in the white Flightsuit®, His sixty-year-old body was sweating and trembling when he looked up and saw Nathan approaching, confidently piloting his personal copter, another rich man's toy.

Jesup's ludicrous flight was over. His master Nathan, all grown up now, had come to take him home. Jesup knew it was over. And as soon as he knew this, he stood, steadied himself against the wind from Nathan's copter blades, swung his right arm overhead, and bolted for the river.

He could see Nathan cursing as he aborted the landing. Jesup capitalized on the head start. He knew where he was going and it wasn't far.

Jesup cast aside all fear of discovery and rose above the pines and live oaks separating the Parker plantation from the Mississippi River. He rose over the refinery towers and got a clear view of the official-looking copters bearing down on him from the north. He tried to remember whether he had ever heard of a runaway slave being harmed. He couldn't recall ever hearing of a runaway slave who had run very far at all.

Nathan dogged him as he rose above the Mississippi River to the top of the towers suspending the Destrehan Bridge. Jesup perched there, looking down at the barges plying North America's great industrial artery and remembered that he too was an industrial giant, more so than Nathan was, really.

Jesup had been an integral part of Parker Petroleum's corporate management, ever since he had earned the MBA so fervently desired by his master. The Great Emancipation had begun about that time, decades before, but Jesup had missed it. He had been too good for emancipation. When Jesup boarded the underground train bound for Harvard all those years ago, he had been all too aware that he was riding on the crest of the latest economic trend.

Slaves were expensive. When unskilled labor was sufficient, it was invariably cheaper to hire workers at minimum wage and let them figure out how to take care of themselves on that paltry sum. Slaves, by contrast, had to be fed and clothed, and the cost of their medical care was outrageous. There were those who neglected their slaves to keep overhead down, but not Walton Parker. Each of his slaves was maintained as meticulously as an expensive piece of machinery. Jesup couldn't have received more lovingly detailed maintenance if he'd been a Maserati.

"If you're not going to look after your valuables, you might as well not have them," Mr. Parker had proclaimed loudly and often to anyone who would listen.

Jesup's master could have saved his breath, because most slaveholders apparently agreed with him. Slaves were being freed at an astonishing rate and, interestingly enough, the slaves who were not freed were uniformly intelligent and well-educated. Their masters had found it cost-prohibitive to maintain a vast staff for menial labor. However, the idea of a business manager of consummate loyalty, one who could be considered to be an extension of oneself, proved seductive to an elite group of men and women who trusted no one but themselves.

The rate of advanced business degrees awarded by the most prestigious universities increased sharply. Everyone wanted to own an MBA.

Walton Parker was no idiot. He had seen intelligence and talent in Jesup before he even learned to speak. He had nurtured Jesup's potential with a fine private education, beginning in preschool. He had planned from the start to complete this education at a hand-picked university. And in between, he had nurtured a relationship between Jesup, the man he had chosen to assist him with building his empire, and Nathan, his only heir. Maybe the two of them together could keep the business afloat when he was gone. Walton Parker was a man who thought way, way ahead.

Had he been asked, Jesup would have preferred to study history, but there was little economic potential for Mr. Parker in owning a slave with a doctorate in colonial American studies, so Jesup quite properly signed up for a major in finance.

He proved to be very, very good, unquestionably good, at his studies. Mr. Parker was not surprised.

Jesup's instructors could not fail to notice him. He invariably sat, dark and slender, in the center front seat. Like all the other students, he monitored the classnote feed streaming to his phone from the professor's microphone and lightboard display. Unlike most other students, he also used the input pad frequently during the lecture, adding his own commentary and noting links to be explored later. He rarely asked questions, but those he asked were succinct and thought-provoking. His professors took notice of the tall young man, they observed the twin rings embedded in the flesh of his index fingers, and they understood why this man's master had invested in his education.

Jesup excelled in the business courses his master chose for him, and he indulged his passion for history at every opportunity. Mr. Parker surely noticed the extra coursework, but he apparently chose to ignore it, since Jesup's work never suffered in his more important classes.

Jesup read. He studied. He tried to work through the inconsistencies.

The Greeks gave birth to democracy, yet they owned slaves and granted citizenship only to the male elite. Marxism had purported to make all citizens equal, but they had lied. Roosevelt had promised to free all American slaves. He had lied, too.

"The health of the entire American economy," he had said, as the country sank into a Depression so deep that freeing the slaves would surely have prompted total economic collapse, "is more important at this critical juncture than is the welfare of a few. For this, I am deeply sorry."

Jesup had read everything available on the Abolitionist movement in the United States. There were those who said that President Lincoln would have freed the slaves if he hadn't been knifed to death by a madman during his inaugural parade. Most of these theorists also believed that a great war would have erupted had he made good on his promises of emancipation.

An even larger contingent of historians believed that President Kennedy would have done away with slavery had he lived. A subset of conspiracy theorists believed that a consortium of slaveholders had arranged to have him shot.

Jesup read all the arguments, time and again, but his own unanswerable question was rarely asked: If Kennedy had truly intended to issue the so-called Emancipation

Proclamation, how could he have served for three years without doing so?

Jesup had finished his undergraduate degree with highest honors and, with equal distinction, earned the MBA so fervently desired by his master. He had returned to New Orleans and become Mr. Parker's personal assistant.

Nathan's father had been the latest in a long line of far-sighted owners of the former Parker Petroleum Industries. The shift from petroleum products to alternative energy technologies had begun in the late 1970s, but Nathan had only recently jettisoned the word "petroleum" from the company title, officially changing it to PPI, Inc.

PPI dominated the burgeoning solar power industry, but Old Man Parker had always kept a few production platforms pumping oil from beneath the Gulf of Mexico, for old times' sake. Even after his father's death, Nathan had never allowed Jesup to shut them down, but he acquiesced to Jesup's opinions on almost all other matters.

Jesup's job performance had suited his first master perfectly from the first. The young man had shown foresight, even vision, in planning business moves. Parker's own son, Nathan, was capable enough. The old man wasn't overly worried about leaving his empire to him. But he was oh-so-grateful that Nathan would have someone like Jesup to guide him.

Throughout his career, Jesup had received compensation that was in many ways comparable to that received by free men in similar positions. He was provided with exquisitely tailored suits. He had a luxurious private apartment in Mr. Parker's spacious home. The domestic staff—all free men and women as slave labor was far too expensive—provided him attentive and unobtrusive service.

Jesup had worked tirelessly. PPI was in many ways the love of his life, for he had refused to marry on principle. Marrying a free woman was unthinkable, and marrying another slave would deprive her of any hope of freedom, ever. Jesup knew that he was too valuable to ever walk free. And the prospect of bringing children into a life of captivity made his blood run cold.

As Mr. Parker grew older, he leaned on Jesup more and more. The old man set corporate policies and Jesup implemented them. In time, Jesup formulated those policies and his aging master read them, recognized the genius in them, and signed the documents making them so.

Nathan graduated with a degree in public relations and was put in charge of sales. He tried hard and performed adequately.

When Mr. Parker died, Nathan was forty-one and Jesup was fifty-six. Nathan was made Chief Executive Officer and Jesup continued as the CEO's assistant, but their titles bore no relationship to reality. Jesup's policies were issued under Nathan's signature and, under the guidance of a strong slave and his well-meaning master, PPI had prospered. And unlike most mega-corporations, PPI had made sure that its employees prospered, too.

The company beefed up fringe benefits, even extending them to minimum-wage employees. Salaries inched upward. PPI became known for meeting and exceeding environmental and safety regulations. Against all predictions, the company continued to prosper. Nathan was interviewed frequently by news organizations seeking the key to his firm's success.

"Nothing," he said, "is as valuable to a company as the knowledge, originality, and enthusiasm embodied in its human staff."

Buoyed by the public response, Nathan gave more interviews. Jesup cautioned against it.

"You are not in control of this situation. Reporters need stories, and they don't much care what they are. Limit your interviews and be damn sure going in that you know what you will and will not be coerced into saying. A pack of reporters is going to eat you alive one day."

Ever the marketing professional, Nathan responded, "The nets give us worldwide free advertising. We couldn't possibly afford this kind of publicity. Well, maybe we could, but this is free."

He gave Jesup the boyish grin that had made his slave love him all those years ago, the same grin that the reporters loved now.

"Jesup, public relations is what I do. You keep your stranglehold on the bottom line. The stockholders love you for it, and God knows I do, too. Please just let me make this one contribution to our success."

Jesup's greatest gift, and perhaps his greatest curse, too, was that he was rarely wrong in business matters. His dire predition was far in the past when a pack of financial reporters assailed Nathan at a convention of energy brokers. Jesup's master had delivered an after-dinner speech chock-full of his favorite homey anecdotes extolling the pleasures of running a family-founded, multi-billion-dollar conglomerate.

Nathan was rare among his contemporaries in giving credit to his employees, even to his slave, for his success. His speech was peppered with "Jesup-isms."

During the question-and-answer period, a reporter who had been waiting patiently for his chance finally got it. "How do you justify your unusually generous worker compensation program to your stockholders?"

Accustomed to this question, Nathan gave his practiced response. "Our employees produce more and stay with us longer because of that very compensation program. Profits are among the best in the industry. Why should we change anything?"

The reporter was not satisfied. "How can you put a value on employee satisfaction or longevity? If an unskilled worker leaves, a replacement can be hired quickly and cheaply. Your logic is faulty in assigning credit for profits to over-generous treatment of workers. Your Jesup is the reason for your profitability."

He waved a copy of PPI's current financial statement. "I have calculated the annual increase in dividends to the average stockholder if PPI reduced its worker benefits to the national average. I assure you that your policies are costing your stockholders a substantial sum."

This statement was indeed unfortunate, because the proceedings were being broadcast live to energy brokers worldwide. Even more unfortunately, many of those physically present owned PPI stock themselves. Jesup was on the net, watching, as they besieged Nathan. He didn't have to switch over to the listings to know that PPI stock values were already inching downward.

This did not concern him, particularly. He knew how to drive them back up. It might take him a while, but he could do it.

At some point, Jesup turned off the visual feed and merely listened to Nathan backpedal away from the angry questions. Later that night, he wept for the man who was not quite his master and who was nearly his son.

After that Nathan spent less time at the office. He took up expensive hobbies. He dated prominent beauties half his age. He bought a Flightsuit®.

One day, during ordinary conversation, Jesup called him "Master Nate." Nathan was horrified.

"Why, Jesup? Do I treat you like a slave? Have I ever treated you like a slave? Maybe Daddy did, but not me."

Jesup merely looked at Nathan's thinning hair and soft skin and white hands. He saw the slight scar near his temple. He loved him, or maybe he just loved the little boy he had been, but he didn't have anything else to say.

Jesup lived even more quietly after that. He worked quietly at his desk, wondering who would run the company when he retired, wondering why he might wish to retire at all. When he needed to speak to Nathan, he politely and invariably called him "Master."

When he shaved in the mornings, he studied the way the white whiskers stood out against his chocolate skin. Yes, he was indeed black, very black. His blackness spoke to the marginal humanity in his masters' ancestors. At the least, they had not raped his grandmothers.

Over time, he further distanced himself from his master, yet his trustworthiness was never in question. Jesup had for so long been an extension of the Parker family that simple customary precautions were no longer taken. That is why Nathan left the Flightsuit® out in full view, and that is how the unfortunate incident occurred.

And that is how Jesup found himself perched high atop the Destrehan Bridge studying the frayed glove of his master's Flightsuit®. He could see Nathan through the glass cabin of his copter and, though he couldn't hear him, he knew that he was pleading with him to come down, to come home, to come back to him. He could hear the federal agents approaching and he knew that they would force him, and not kindly, to go home and live the life he was born to live.

It was over. His ludicrous flight was over. And when Jesup knew that it was really over, he stepped gracefully from the bridge.

The suit's safety features kicked in and held him motionless in mid-air. He swung himself head-down and still the suit supported him. But when he clasped his right hand to his chest and extended his left hand downward, his body began to drop. The mangled left glove did not respond to the position analyzer's insistent demands that it exert a repulsive force sufficient to balance gravity.

Instead, his bare black hand, slaves' ring firmly embedded, allowed gravity to drag him downward. As he accelerated, he knew that the federal agents were cursing and that Nathan was weeping.

Jesup fell down the only path that he had ever chosen for himself. He plunged downward, knowing that from the moment the mahogany waters closed over him until the moment his body was captured by the sediments beneath, he would be free from the directions of any mortal and subject only to the whims of Nature and of Nature's God.

"Jesup's Flight" came close to being published in a small speculative fiction publication about twelve years ago. The editor liked it, but he asked if I'd be willing to do a rewrite. I was willing. I always appreciate being edited. As an artist, I feel more free to take risks when I know that someone I trust will tell me when I've gone too far. As a wordsmith who is serious about the English language, I know that my grammar and style are not always flawless, and I'd far rather have my editor detect my errors than my readers.

Unfortunately, this editor wanted to take the revision of "Jesup's Flight" one step further than I could bear. He wanted me to change the ending and let Jesup live.

I desperately wanted to see my story go out into the world. By this time, I'd been submitting my short stories and seeing them come home, rejected, for about sixteen years.

(Have I mentioned that I can be stubborn to the point of possible mental illness?) I thought the story was a good one, and I'd had the backhanded positive feedback that comes with complimentary rejections from some of the biggest names in the business.

I did my best to come up with a satisfying ending for this story that would allow Jesup to live, and I was motivated by more than the hope of publication. I loved Jesup. I wanted him to live.

I just couldn't do it. I wish I could tell you that my motivations were entirely noble...that I wasn't willing to sell out. Those motivations surely came into play, but the truth was far simpler and less high-minded. I just couldn't think of any other way to end this story.

What, really, are Jesup's options? After having come to an honest understanding of his life as a captive of a lesser man, is he really going to go home and live the life that man wants him to live? Is he going to rebel completely and go to prison, or wherever it is that this version of America sends its recalcitrant runaway slaves? Even with his formidable intellect, does he have any hope of finding a way to live out his life in freedom? Perhaps if he hadn't been burdened with that formidable intellect, he might have been able to fool himself into believing there was a way to free himself, but Jesup knows better. Sixty years as a slave have taught him that he would rather be free for the few moments it takes him to fall to his death than to live for thirty more years as someone else's possession.

Because I wasn't willing to take Jesup's freedom from him, his story has remained imprisoned in my computer for all these years. I'm so grateful for the opportunity to show it to you.

-Mary Anna

AND NOW WE RETURN TO THE MYSTERY FICTION THAT I LOVE SO WELL...

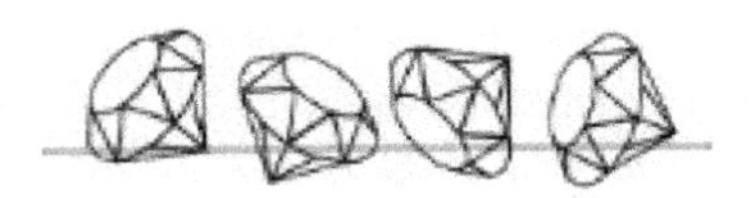

CALLY'S STORY

In case it is not already apparent in the fact that I've written all these stories and gathered them together for you to read, I adore the short story as an art form. Alfred Hitchcock and Isaac Asimov were prolific editors of the short story anthologies I devoured as a child. I was, and am, ever so grateful to them both for providing me with such a wealth of reading material. And they had such good taste! Even now, I still remember and savor some of the best plots in their collections. I also really enjoyed the commentary they added before and after the stories in their anthologies, so I am emulating the masters in the way I have constructed this book.

My first formal training as a fiction writer was a course in short story writing taught by a well-known and highly esteemed writer, Ellen Douglas. After taking that course, my writing gravitated toward two genres—literary fiction and speculative fiction—that are not as different as popular misconceptions might have you believe. I have already shared with you my frustration over not being able to interest an editor in publishing that work.

One of the last of the speculative fiction stories that I wrote before writing Artifacts *was published in 2003 was called "Last Island," and I think it might be of special interest to those of you who are familiar with my mysteries.*

You see, "Last Island" became a small part of Artifacts.

All of my Faye Longchamp mysteries, beginning with Artifacts, *have a distinctive structure. Because*

I write about an archaeologist, the past is an important part of the present-day stories, yet a dry recitation of a historical lesson would kill those stories dead. Listening to the voice of a living human being is just so much more interesting. In my books, I create characters who lived in the past that my archaeologist is researching, then I use letters and diaries and oral histories and folk tales to let those long-dead people speak in their own voices. As it turns out, one of the historical stories told in Artifacts, *the reminiscences of the slave girl Cally, began as a fantasy short story, "Last Island," that I hacked up and reassembled in a format that fit my mystery-in-process.*

When I began assembling this collection, my thought was to resurrect "Last Island" in its original form, publishing it back-to-back with the reminiscences of Cally from Artifacts. *Since I'm still a scientist at heart, I loved the idea of comparing the two stories to see how they differed and, hopefully, to determine why they differed.*

Unfortunately, I found that I was no longer happy with "Last Island," and I refuse to subject my cherished readers to it.

(You can thank me any time.)

Maybe it's because I've internalized the story in its new form, and I find it jarring to read the earlier version. Or maybe it's just because I've matured as a writer. In re-reading it, I noticed a few important details that I'll share with you, but I'm otherwise going to let it rest in my files, unread by anyone but me.

In the original story, the narrator was a slave girl named Cassy, because my intent was to do a modern retelling of the Greek story of Cassandra, the slave girl who was cursed to see the future yet never be able to convince anyone to avoid the coming doom. It was intended to be a fantasy story, so there was obviously some supernatural content that didn't survive in the Artifacts *version of the tale, including childhood instances of precognition and a description of how she learned voodoo from another slave.*

All those magical things disappeared in an instant when I used a few keystrokes to turn Cassy into Cally, then obliterated her childhood training as a voodoo mambo. What is left is a story about someone who believes her dreams tell the future, but the reader is left to decide whether she has unnatural powers.

Readers often tell me that they loved Cally's story in Artifacts, *flipping forward to read the installments back-to-back, as a single story. Here, for the first time, I've printed that story in just that way.*

And now I believe I've said enough. It's time to let Cally do the talking.

-Mary Anna

CALLY'S STORY

Originally published as part of *Artifacts*

Excerpt from oral history of Cally Stanton, recorded by the Federal Writer's Project, 1935

I've been a slave and I've been free. I've been mistress of a big plantation, and of its master, too. I was there when the water pulled itself far, far from the beaches at Last Isle and I saw the wind blow the water back. It rolled over Last Isle and washed away the big hotel and all the rich white people, and their slaves, too. Nobody ever gave much thought to the slaves that died on Last Isle, but I did. I was a slave on Last Isle and I was there when the big storm roared in and washed the whole island away.

You could say I saw the big storm twice. I saw it in my sleep a long time before it happened. I guess I should have tried to warn all those rich folks, but they wouldn't have listened to a skinny half-grown slave. Still, I knew death was watching over us. My dreams ain't never once been wrong.

My worst dream came first, when I was a slip of a girl. I saw people sick and dying. Miss Mariah, the Master's mama, was laid up in the bed alongside the first Missus, and my mama was tending them. Then Mama took sick and they laid her on the sleeping porch and there was nobody in my dream to tend them but me.

And that's just how it happened. When the fever came, I took care of all three sweet ladies, but the typhoid carried them away, along with half the slaves.

When the fever passed, the Master sent all the house slaves to the fields. 'Twasn't any other way to get the harvest in, not with so many field hands dead and in their graves. My skinny six-year-old self wouldn't have been much good at picking cotton, so they gave me the whole Big House to dust and sweep and clean. I was so good at keeping house that I got to where I knew the Master wanted coffee before he did.

I liked to bring him a hot cup in his office. He was a handsome man and I never, before or since, saw the like of his golden hair. I was about grown before I found out he wasn't nothing but a mean man.

Lots of folks said the second Missus was stupid, but I knew her better than they did. She wasn't stupid. She was a Yankee.

She took to me from the start, saying I was pretty and I had elegant bones. She said I was smart, too, and she wanted to teach me to dress and talk, so's I could be a proper lady's maid. Maybe I'm smart. I think I am. But only a Yankee could look at my skin and my hair and, yes, Lord, even my bones, without wondering who my daddy was. I don't rightly know who my daddy was, but there wasn't never but one white man on the place and that was her husband.

The new Missus kept herself busy by keeping me busy. I sponged her down with cool water—she didn't take to our weather—and I fetched her drinks. A little bourbon made her forget how the heat made her corsets stick to her skin. A little more bourbon made her forget that the Master married her for her money.

It wasn't hard work to take care of the second Missus and her bourbon. There was nothing to tote and carry, nothing except her chamber pot, and I never had to do any mopping or dusting outside her bedchamber. Nobody was allowed to give me anything else to do, because what if I was chopping squash for the cook and the Missus needed her lady's maid?

The Big House was a nice place to work, lots better than the kitchen or, good Lord...the fields. The Missus' bedchamber felt cool to me, with the breezes coming in the tall windows and blowing the lace curtains around. There was just one bad thing about the Big House. The Master was there, and before long he noticed I was growing up.

I have lived a long ninety-six years. In all that time, I never hated anybody but one man: my Master, Andrew LaFourche. I never hated anybody in my life before the Master dragged me into an empty room and locked the door.

The Missus never noticed when my clothes was messed up and my mouth was bloody. Maybe my skin's dark enough so the bruises didn't show. I don't know. But she never noticed. Or she made like she didn't notice.

Later on, he learned to hit me so he didn't leave marks. And I learned not to feel anything much at all. Time and again, I dreamed that he was going to come to a bad end and that I was going to make it happen. There was a heap of comfort in that.

The Missus always chirked up when her son, Mister Courtney Stanton, came to see her. Mister Courtney was a fine-looking man. His hair was even prettier than the master's, the color of sweet corn, more white than yellow. And shiny, good Lord.

Mister Courtney decided he wanted to live near his mama, so he bought a fine plantation named Innisfree, slaves and all. It was right next door to one of the Master's tobacco plantations. He bought Last Isle, too, though I couldn't imagine why, not when it wasn't fit for farming. I didn't say nothing, 'cause I already told you how much stock was put in the things a skinny slave girl had to say. And, for once, I was wrong.

The first thing Mister Courtney did was lease half the island to one of his Yankee friends to build a hotel on. That foolish Yankee paid him more for the lease than Mister Courtney had paid for the island to begin with, so it made him money right away. It would've kept making him money for the rest of his life, if things had turned out different, so I was always glad I never told him what I thought of his investment.

The next thing he did was set to work on the Big House at Innisfree. Nobody had lived in that house for nigh onto five years—nobody except for possums and bats—and the roof had taken to leaking. Folks said Mister Courtney waded into his new house—right beside the slaves—to help shoo out the possums and mop out the mud. It was a scandal the way he acted, the white folks said. And their house servants heard every word.

Some said Mr. Courtney had bought a cobbler who did nothing all day but make shoes for the field hands. Some said he'd torn down the old slave cabins and built new brick ones. If all the stories were true, then Mr. Courtney had invited the black folk to move themselves right into the Big House and make themselves at home. And to help themselves to all his money while they were at it.

No, those were tall tales, but I knew a true tale and I wasn't telling. Mister Courtney was thinking about freeing his slaves. I heard him tell his Mama with my own ears. I didn't believe he'd do it, but the idea of belonging to somebody who'd even give it a thought made me dizzy. Thinking about my own Master made me dizzy, and sick to my stomach, too. He wasn't a man to set his slaves free. No, sir. I would belong to that man until I died or he did.

Going to Last Isle was Mister Courtney's idea and he always felt bad about it. It came about because he came to visit with his mama, like he always did, and she'd had too much bourbon, like she always did. She was crying, because that's what the bourbon did to her, and he asked her why didn't she go with him to the grand opening of the new hotel his business partner was opening on Last Isle? I can still hear his sweet voice saying, "I hear it has every amenity."

When he said that, I stopped my dusting and leaned up against the window seat to free up all my strength for praying.

Please, Lord, let her go to Last Isle and let her take me.

I'd be out of the Master's reach for weeks. I held my breath.

The Missus kept sipping her bourbon, but she nodded her head yes and I was a happy woman.

It wasn't long before the Missus found a way to spoil my happiness. I remember the day, I remember it well. I was packing her suitcase and loving my work.

I'm going away from this place, I'd say to myself while the flatiron got hot.

The Master can keep his ugly face right here, I'd say when I was laying her underclothes in the travel trunk.

I'll just keep the Missus drunk and have me a fine old time.

But I should have got her drunk before we left, because when I went to heat the flatiron back up, I heard her talking to him.

"Really, dear, I wish you would go with me. How could I enjoy myself properly without my husband?"

The tears ran down my face. It surprised me. It'd been a long time since I took the trouble to cry.

I prayed a lot the whole rest of that day.

Don't let the Master go with us to Last Isle, I prayed while I brushed the Missus's everyday poplin, and while I swept off the sun porch, and when I lay in my bed that night. *Don't let him go.*

I thought I'd hear those words all night—*Don't let him go!*—but I didn't. I slept a good sleep and I had a good dream and I woke up singing, because I knew the Master was going to die.

I didn't rightly see how it would happen. My dreams don't always come clear. All I could see was gray water and foamy waves, and somehow I knew I was on Last Isle, not in the Big House on Joyeuse Island. The Missus was whinkering in my dream, because the Master was dead and I did it. And I wasn't afraid, no, I wasn't afraid any more. I wasn't afraid of being slapped to the ground. I wasn't afraid of a fist in my belly. I wasn't even afraid of hanging for murder. I was glad he was dead, glad I killed him. And I had a notion I wouldn't hang. I didn't know how, but I was thinking I might kill my master and walk free.

❖ ◆ ❖ ◆ ❖

I'm a good liar. Belonging to somebody else can surely bring out the liar in you.

"Yes, ma'am, you are surely right. It's not fitting for a lady to go off without her husband to take care of her," I'd say when I carried their breakfast in.

She'd straighten her bedcovers over her fat belly and cut her eyes over at the Master.

When the Missus took her nap, I'd find the Master and walk past him, swinging my skirts. "I never saw a hotel," I'd say.

"It's not a hotel. It's a glorified boarding house," he'd say, cutting his possum-eyes away from me.

I'd just swing my skirts some more and say, "I don't blame you for being afraid. A big storm might rise up and blow you to kingdom come. And your purty wife, too."

There. I'd told the truth. If he didn't listen, it was none of my affair.

"Folks say that Last Isle's a pretty place to take a walk," I'd say, brushing a piece of lint off his pants leg. "Sure wish I had somebody to take a walk with." Then I'd lean over and give him a good look down my dress. "Somebody handsome."

We kept after him, the Missus and me, until he packed his bags. Mister Courtney didn't care for the Master, so he didn't go with us, after all. Before long, the Master, the Missus, and me were on a steamboat headed for Last Isle.

The hotel there was even fancier than the Big House at Innisfree, and it wasn't snugged up under a shady grove, like our Big House at Joyeuse. It sat right out on the beach, plain as you please.

The sun shone funny that day on Last Isle, like it knew a secret. It made the real world look like one of my dreams. I was standing on the beach, afraid of the way the sun made my shadow look, when I heard an old man say, "I've seen weather like this. There's a hurricane coming"—he pronounced it 'hurrikan'—"I'd bet forty acres on it."

Another man said, "This is no place to wait out a hurricane. This island hardly pokes out of the water. I'm going home to Mississippi, where I can walk without getting my feet wet."

I watched those men head back to the hotel and set their slaves to packing. Both their families and their slaves were off Last Isle that same afternoon. I have always prayed they were all safe at home when the storm hit.

Not many had sense enough to leave. I had the sense, but I was bound to stay. This storm was gonna kill my Master for me.

The Missus heard talk about the storm coming, and she wanted to leave, but I shut her up. "Ain't gonna be no storm, ma'am. Look at that sun shine."

She kept up her whining, but the Master didn't say nothing. I think he had boat tickets to get us out the next day. I won't never know for sure, but he was a smart man. Those tickets didn't do any of us a bit of good. The storm hit that very night.

Now I've seen thunderstorms and I've seen hurricanes. Thunderstorms come up fast and loud and dark. They make plenty of light and noise, but unless you get lightning-struck, you'll get through a thunderstorm.

Hurricanes are different. I have never felt a building shake like that hotel did and I have never, before or since, heard the banshee cry in the wind. Before that night, I never saw a tree lean over sideways and snap in two. When the water pulled back away from the island, I knew it was bad. The water was gathering together, so it could throw itself on us all at once.

Have you ever watched Death come for you?

We were on the top floor of that hotel, so we could see the big wave coming a long time before it hit. The Master was standing at the window and I was behind him, looking over his shoulder. The Missus was curled up in bed, just crying. The big wave was gathering and the storm was shaking the hotel harder and harder when it happened.

The window busted right open. I hid my face in my hands and waited for the glass to hit me, but it never did.

The wind hadn't blown the window in. It had sucked it out into the night. And the Master stood there, teetering at the windowsill.

Later on, I thought maybe I wasn't a murderer after all, because I didn't think about what I did. I didn't think to myself, *This man beat me and had his way with me and he deserves to die.* No, my hands just reached up by themselves and pushed him out of the broken window.

The storm swallowed him up. I turned around and there sat the Missus, looking at me. She saw what I did. I know she did. But she never said nothing, because that's when the big wave hit.

The big wave washed right up to the sill of that broken window. Folks on the bottom floors never had a chance. The wind was coming in hard, but I thought the building would hold. Maybe it would have, if that first wave had been the only one.

The Good Book says a house built on sand will fall and a house built on rock will stand. That worries me, because I don't think there's a rock big enough to stand on in all of Florida. There wasn't nothing on Last Isle to build on but sand, and I was there when it all tumbled down.

The hotel came apart, flinging splinters and boards far and wide. The wind was like a wolf breaking open a log to get at the little rabbit inside, and the little rabbit was me. The shrieking storm drowned out the Missus and her screaming. That was good, because it meant I could forget her and save my own rabbit skin.

The walls fell around me. As the water carried me off, two dresser drawers floated by and I grabbed one. I don't know why, but I shoved the other drawer over to the

Missus and helped her grab hold. Then we floated out the window and watched the hotel pieces wash away.

The Missus hung on to that dresser drawer with more spunk than I figured. I knew I could get through just about anything, but the Missus couldn't get to the outhouse without a buggy and a span of horses. While we were trying not to drown, she rambled on about wanting to see her son one last time, and she cussed the Master's dead body. She cussed him over and over, until her curses wormed their way into my ears and my brain, just like the everlasting wind. She took on something terrible about what he did to me and to my mama.

And he thought he was so smart and his wife wouldn't never know.

Every now and then a big wave would break over her face and she'd be quiet, because nobody can fling curses out of a mouth full of saltwater. I myself didn't have much to say, so we'd float quiet-like for awhile.

Then, after she'd spent a few minutes spitting saltwater, the Missus would get her mouth clear. She'd start cussing her husband's dead body some more, but I thought she was jumping the gun a little. We didn't really know he was dead, did we?

I hoped he wasn't. Not yet. I wanted him to float around in that black water, just like we were, getting beat up side the head with floating tree limbs and trying to catch a breath that wasn't half sea water. The whole time we fought that storm, I hoped he was suffering, too. Then, when the storm finally slacked up, I went back to wanting him dead.

It was dark when the wind died down, but the moon was bright and I could see a tree poking out of a patch of sand that hardly rose out of the water. I set out swimming for it, dragging my dresser drawer behind me. I was glad for the Sunday afternoons before Miss Mariah died when she took me swimming in the salty Gulf. I wasn't glad a bit for the Missus's company, because her spunk left her when the storm did.

She whined and she fussed and I had to just about drag her fat self through the water. Then she wouldn't climb up the tree with me. She was afraid to let go of the drawer, because it saved her life and she might need it again. I threw up my hands and left her, holding her drawer with one hand and a tree trunk with the other.

I sat in my tree and let the water drop off me. There wasn't a breath of wind and the moon shone like it had a secret. I wasn't surprised when the wind came back from the other direction.

I wrapped my arms and legs around the tree trunk and wished for my dresser drawer. The Missus was hollering for me, but I couldn't go to her. If I got down out of that tree, I would never see the light of another day. I didn't need a dream to tell me that.

Hours later...a lifetime later...the storm played out and the sun came up along about the same time. I could see a long ways from my tree, but there wasn't much to see, just a few other treetops. Last Isle was gone.

I figured rescue boats would come, since the hotel had been full of rich people. There wasn't any other way I was getting out of there alive, so I figured I might as well stay in my tree and hope for a boat. I was hoping hard, because my dream said the Master was going to die. It didn't say anything about me or the Missus.

Maybe hoping works. When the boat came, I was hungry and thirsty and bug-bit, but I wasn't dead. I wasn't alone, either. When the sun got high on that first day, I looked down at the bottom of my tree, where the storm had piled trash and sand and tree limbs. The Missus was laying there, pale and slack-mouthed. I felt like she still needed someone to fetch things for her. Just someone to take care of her. But I couldn't do her any good, not now, so I stayed put. We waited together, the Missus and me.

When the rescuers came, the captain asked me who I belonged to. I opened my mouth to say they were dead and shut it again. I'd lived through a hurricane, but I was scared to death of the auction. I opened my mouth again and said, "I belong to Mister Courtney. Mister Courtney Stanton. He's the master at Innisfree. And now, I guess, he's the master at Joyeuse, too."

Living in the Big House at Joyeuse after the hurricane and I killed my Master felt like I'd died and gone to heaven, but it didn't make Mister Courtney happy. Sometimes, he sat at his desk and unlocked the drawer where he kept his business things. Then he laid bills of sale for all his people across the desk, calling them by name as he sorted through their papers.

"Rufus. Sallie. Beau. Scipio. Ora." Then he would set one paper to the side, away from the others, and say, "Cally." After a minute, he'd go back to counting his people. There were plenty of them, since he inherited Joyeuse because the Master didn't leave any children. Well, he left me, but I didn't count.

Mister Courtney's Mama must have told him that his stepfather, the Master, was my daddy. Knowing that, a decent man like Mister Courtney couldn't treat me like a slave. He gave me a room in the Big House and, even though he never asked me to run his household, I did. It needed doing, and I knew how.

Once he told me he wanted to set all his slaves free. When I caught my breath, I asked him why he didn't go ahead and do it. I can still hear what he said.

"Because I'm afraid." He fingered through the bills of sale laid across his desk and said, "I'm afraid of what will happen to them, and I'm afraid of what will happen to me."

It took a long time for the War to touch us at Joyeuse. Mister Courtney didn't go away to fight, on account of his lame leg. Truth be told, I never noticed his limp until I came to live with him, because he carried himself like a prince. When he spoke, he fastened his blue eyes on you so direct that you hardly noticed whether the sun was shining. You certainly didn't notice anything so paltry as a weak leg.

I know you can tell that I was in love with him. In the seventy years since, I never met anyone who could hold a candle to him so I've been alone, but we had a few good years together, my Courtney and me. It took some time for us to forget that he was my Master. He surely forgot it quicker than I did. But we lived together in his house and I took care of things for him and I was the only person in the world he could talk to. I was his wife in every way but one. In the end it was up to me to show him that I could be his wife in that way, as well.

I think it wasn't just Courtney's leg that was weak. I think it was his heart, too. When he left us, it was sudden. He came riding in from the fields, holding his chest. I tried to help him off his horse, but he fell. I was a skinny thing in those days, but I'm proud to say I caught him.

I fixed him a bed out on the porch where it was cool and he was comfortable there, but right away he sent me inside to look for a box hidden in his desk.

"It's your Christmas present," he said, "but I think I need to give it to you now."

It was a chatelaine, all made out of gold. It hung at my waist and held my keys and my scissors and my thimble and everything else that the lady of a great plantation needed to get through the day. I said I couldn't think of any gift I'd like better, then he pulled a gold ring out of his pocket. He'd had it made with a funny little loop on the side.

"You can wear it on your finger when it's safe, but you know that little ring could put you in jail. The law won't let you be my wife. When strangers come around, you wear that ring on your chatelaine. You understand, don't you?"

His voice got stronger when he talked about that little ring, and I began to hope he would pull through. But when I said, "Yes. I understand," he settled down and got weaker again.

He put the ring on my finger and said "I do," and made sure I said it, too. Then he said, fainter still, "A wedding present. What shall I give you?"

The word "Freedom," came out of my mouth before I thought and he said, "Oh, Cally, I tore up your paper long ago."

"Not just for me," I said. "For everybody."

So I fetched the papers out of his desk and helped him write "Freed in consideration of years of faithful labor," across the face of every one of them.

The next day, my precious Courtney left me alone, five months pregnant and responsible for a hundred new-made freedmen.

I saved my favorite story till last. I always laugh when I remember the day the Yankees came to liberate the slaves on Joyeuse Island. They were naturally more gape-jawed when they found us already free.

Courtney always said I was a charming liar. Well, I did him proud that day. I knew it wouldn't be safe to let anybody, not the Yankees or anybody, know that we didn't have a master any more. The laws weren't good back then and the courts were even worse. Somebody was liable to come take the land—*my* land—and make my workers farm it for just about nothing.

So I told them the master and his wife had gone to Tallahassee that very day to pledge their allegiance to the Yankee flag. Then I showed them young Courtney, my baby, and made sure they knew that my job was to take care of the master's heir. I forgot to mention that young Courtney was a girl and not entitled to own anything in her own name. I also forgot to mention that she wasn't white, so she wasn't entitled to anything in this life at all.

I practiced that lie on the Yankees, then I told it to the people who wrote up the deed. By the time Courtney was bigger and people noticed she was a girl, nobody gave the deed much thought again until just last year when they used my old lies as an excuse to take part of her inheritance away. Courtney fought them. She fought them hard, because the women in our family are tough. We could chew the heads off a barrel of nails if we had to. We lost that land, but we'll get it back.

And we'll always have Joyeuse. Men come and go. They go to war and die. They get diseases and die. They meet other women and leave, then you wish they would die. But home is forever.

Mark my words: Take care of your home. Keep its roof fixed, and the taxes paid, and never mortgage it. Then you'll always have a place to go.

And let me tell you another thing. Don't ever hide anything so well that you can't never find it again. When the Federals came, I sunk my chatelaine and all the table silver in a cow pond because I was damned if I'd see the

Yankees get it. I have shed many tears over my treasures ever since then, because I never found them. Sometimes I send my little great-granddaughter out to dig for the precious wedding ring that Courtney gave me.

I think I'll send her out there now. It's always good to keep little folks busy.

As it turned out, Cally was not finished telling me stories. She makes another appearance in my fourth Faye Longchamp mystery Findings.

It was really good to spend time with her again.

-Mary Anna

Excerpt from
WOUNDED EARTH

People frequently ask me why I write about an archaeologist, since I'm not one. My routine answer to that one is that people think engineers are boring. (But we're not!)

Nevertheless, there's a lot of validity to the old adage, "Write what you know." I do a great deal of research to make Faye's adventures as accurate as possible. Certainly, knowledgeable souls will find places in the books where I deviate from fact. Sometimes it is out of ignorance, and sometimes it is because I needed to tell an exciting story, but I do try hard to make those exciting events plausible. In one of my books, though, I got the chance to tell the story of a woman whose job is very like one that I held for quite a long time.

The protagonist of my thriller Wounded Earth *is Larabeth McLeod, the founder and owner of a successful environmental consulting firm. I made Larabeth a biochemist, not an engineer, because people think engineers are boring. (We're not, but I already said that.) Much of her day-to-day work life, however, is based on work I have done. I definitely had to do a lot of research for this book, since it involves a lunatic who is planning nuclear disaster, but I was much closer to my comfort zone than I usually am when I'm writing.*

Larabeth is also a devoted mother of a daughter. I am that, too, twice over, and perhaps this book tells a different story than it might have, if not for the fact that I was pregnant with my third child when I wrote it.

Unlike me, Larabeth has never met her daughter, but I was able to channel my own experience as a mother into her motivation and her pain. People tell me that they enjoy this woman who is smart and strong and capable, yet she is utter putty in the hands of a man willing to harm her child.

Here is an excerpt from the full-length thriller Wounded Earth, offered as a gift for those of you who have read and enjoyed the short works in this volume. Some stories need to be short and some stories need to be long. One of a writer's joys is figuring out what shape a story wants to take. Enjoy!

-Mary Anna

Excerpt From *WOUNDED EARTH*

by Mary Anna Evans

Chapter 1

Summer 1995, New Orleans, Louisiana

Babykiller was meticulous in all things. It was his defining quality. Attention to detail was the key to longevity in his chosen profession, and Babykiller had been in business a long, long time.

Most of his competitors from the early days were dead or in prison, and he couldn't claim responsibility for all their misfortune. No, they had simply chosen a dangerous line of work. He was well on his way to outliving a second generation and he was considering retirement. At least he had been, before the oncologist's verdict. Retirement planning seemed so futile when death was certain.

Babykiller had created a life out of certainties. He left nothing to chance. He made no mistakes—at least, he made no mistakes that were obvious to the cretins who purchased his services. He had built a seamless organization that ran like a Volvo. It was reliable. It required little maintenance. It was safe. It was boring as hell. Even if his organization survived him—and he cared very little whether it did or not—it was a plain-vanilla sort of legacy for a man of his caliber.

Babykiller had more money than he could have spent in a normal lifetime. He had more than a fair share of cunning. And he had a long list of scores to settle with the world before he took his leave of it. It was time to retire and focus his considerable attentions on something more interesting. Or someone more interesting.

Babykiller had kept extensive files on his target for years, ever since he began thinking of retirement. He had videotapes and audiotapes. An accordion file labeled "Bio-Heal Environmental Services" held her company's annual financial reports, one for each year she'd been in business. His clipping file bulged with articles dating to her first appearance on the cover of *New Orleans Business News.*

Larabeth McLeod had enjoyed good press from the start, for the usual reasons. She was an easy interview. Her field, environmental science, was red-hot. She was witty and down-to-earth. Her strong jawline made for good photographs. Reporters loved her.

She smiled out of the manila folder at him, wearing her success like a crisply tailored suit. He replaced the clippings in reverse chronological order and closed the file over her elegantly sculpted face. He remembered that face. He had cherished it long before the photographers fell in love. He had seen it contorted in pain, spattered in blood.

He would like very much to see it that way again.

Larabeth wouldn't ordinarily have answered the phone. That's why she had a secretary—to screen calls she was too busy to take. And she was too busy. The morning had been frittered away on tasks that should have stayed buried in the middle of her to-do list. It was only Wednesday, and it was already clear she'd have to work on Saturday if she hoped to catch up.

She checked her watch. Yes, the morning was gone. Blown to hell, in fact. If she didn't leave in ten minutes, she would be late for a televised appearance that her publicity people had spent weeks arranging. But the phone was ringing and it was her personal line. Only her biggest clients and a handful of key contacts had that number. If she missed this call, she might well regret it. Of course, if she took this call and missed her speech, she would regret that. Or if she took the call and brushed off an important client in order to leave in time, she might regret that, too. A no-win situation.

Or, she thought, perhaps it's a no-lose situation. It could be hard to tell the difference. She answered the phone on the sixth ring.

"Larabeth McLeod, your voice is as lovely on the telephone as it is on television. Or in person, as a matter of fact." The man's voice was unfamiliar. She fumbled for the list of people who had the private number. It was short, no more than fifteen people. Eight of them were women. If she stayed cool, she could figure out who this guy was without insulting him.

"You're so kind to say that," she said, scratching Oskar Weinbaum, Guillaume Langlois, and Manuel Ganzerla off the list of possibilities. This man had absolutely no accent.

"Not kind at all, just truthful. Your speaking voice is matter-of-fact, honest, and very feminine. You're a shrewd enough businesswoman to recognize it as an asset."

Larabeth laughed politely, scratching the next three names off her list. Terry, James, and Guy were old friends. They didn't bother with flattery. That left one candidate: Joe Don Simpkins, a middle-aged oil mogul and a major prospective client. Joe Don's cowboy drawl was too broad to be fake. She threw the list down. Who was this guy and how did he get her number?

"I won't keep you long. You've got an important speech to make. I just wanted to tell you personally how... impressed I've been with your meteoric career. What other lowly Army medic could have become a hotshot bio-chemist so quickly? I should call you Doctor Larabeth, shouldn't I? Or maybe just Doc. And your business—why, not so many years ago you were running a one-woman shop out of your garage. Now you're on the brink of going multi-national. Congratulations, my dear."

Larabeth was taken aback, but only momentarily. "Who is this? Are the personal details supposed to make me think you know me? Everything you've said has been in the papers a dozen times. I'm hanging up now. As you said, I have an appointment to keep." Her hand moved to break the connection.

"Keep your wits about you, Doc," the voice purred. "I know you can. You're level-headed enough to kill a man who's in the process of slicing you up. I'd say you were someone to be reckoned with. Almost my equal. Almost."

Larabeth's hand froze just short of the telephone. She had never talked about that. Not to reporters. Not to anyone. That incident was buried somewhere in her military records. Maybe somewhere inside her, too, but she hadn't checked lately.

"I would like you, Larabeth, if I liked anybody, and I do admire you. I think you understand my dilemma. It's damn unfulfilling to dream and plan and act when no one has the capacity to understand you. It's a burden being superior to those around you. You know that, don't you? Well, you may not like my plans, Larabeth, but I've chosen you to share them with me. Good-bye, Doc. Stay close to the phone."

Larabeth hung up slowly and looked at her watch. She still had time to make it, if she stashed this disturbing incident in the back of her mind, for now. She rushed out past her assistant, Norma, who held her jacket and briefcase.

"Your VIP pass and cell phone are in the outer pocket," Norma said, walking Larabeth to the elevator, "and I made sure you had the proper shade of lipstick to match your outfit. Bittersweet, I think. I just love having a woman boss."

Larabeth looked down at her suit. "This color? Bittersweet? Decayed pumpkin is what I'd call it."

"Whatever," Norma said. "Anyway, it looks great on you."

Larabeth grinned her thanks. "I hope I look okay for a woman on the far side of forty. Listen, Norma, I just had a scary phone call from some kind of a nut. Do me a favor and call J.D. Hatten." She grabbed a sticky-note and scrawled a number on it. "He's a private detective and we go way back. Tell him to call me this afternoon." The elevator doors closed between them.

Norma studied her own plump legs. She herself was also on the far side of forty and looked it, unquestionably. Larabeth might owe her brunette pageboy to L'Oreal and her resemblance to Sigourney Weaver to God, but her slender waist could only come from discipline. Norma sucked in her gut, promising herself fifty sit-ups when she got home. Or maybe after dinner. She hurried to call J.D. Hatten, wondering why Larabeth knew his number by heart.

"Well, as best as I can tell, I have once again avoided embarrassing the firm," Larabeth announced as she strode into the office and set her briefcase down with a thunk. Norma noticed that Larabeth's hair was slightly mussed, her makeup could use freshening, and her skirt was wrinkled across the lap. She still looked great but she was, thank goodness, human.

"Did your speech go well?" Norma asked.

"It was okay, just the usual spiel. You know, 'We've all got to work together to save this beautiful planet.' Everybody wants to hear what they think they already know."

"It's usually safest to give people what they want," Norma said, handing her a sheaf of pink message slips.

"It's good for business," Larabeth said, "but it does get old." She rifled through the pink slips and sighed.

The afternoon was half-gone when Larabeth reached the last message. She'd averted a half-dozen crises and initiated yet another round of telephone tag with the other callers. She patted herself on the back. It could have been worse.

As she read the final slip, her self-congratulatory mood faded. Norma, ordinarily so cautious with her message-taking, had neither taken down the name of the caller nor recorded his number. The message said:

Enjoyed your speech, Doc. It was informative, even if you did water down your topic for the comfort of the masses. By the way, you look great in orange. Stay close to the phone.

Norma had added a note saying:

(Larabeth—This man insisted that I take his message verbatim. He wouldn't leave his name, but he said he was a friend of yours. I thought he might be J.D. Hatten, since we're still waiting for his return call.)

Larabeth read the note again. *Enjoyed your speech, Doc.* The crank caller had called her "Doc". An air conditioner breeze blew cold on her cheek. After a moment, the slip of paper fell from her fingers. She checked her fingernails with the practiced eye of a former medic and found the blue tinge of mild shock. She closed her eyes. It was important to think rationally.

How could he know what color she was wearing? For that matter, how could he know that her message had been "watered down"? Her speech wouldn't be broadcast for hours. He could only know these things if he'd been there. She willed herself not to tremble. So what if someone drove out to Audubon Park and took his place under an oak tree? So what if that someone stood there and listened to her admittedly insipid speech? Hundreds of others had done the same thing.

This was different. Larabeth's hand began trembling again. She couldn't stop her hand from shaking, but she could still use it to take action. She activated the intercom.

"Norma, have we heard from J.D.?"

"Not unless he was the one who left that weird message."

"No. In fact, he'll want to ask you about that. I'm certain it was the same nut. I refuse to panic for no reason, but I'll feel better when I get J.D.'s opinion. Would you hold my calls for the afternoon?"

"You bet."

Larabeth switched off the intercom and sat quietly for a moment. She didn't know what to do and it was an odd feeling. She always knew what to do. If she were ever forced to describe herself in a single word, "competent" would be the word. If she were allowed a few more words for self-description, "businesslike", "practical", and "diligent" would come immediately to mind.

She couldn't remember having time to waste. Not when there was a business to be built and nurtured. And not, before that, when there were classes to take, and research to do, and a doctorate to pursue. And certainly, before that, there had been no time to waste in Vietnam, when men might die for want of the medications in her hands.

This feeling came upon her rarely, this paralyzed confusion. It struck her once a year, maybe twice, and she just sat at her desk and looked at her telephone, her computer, her to-do list. She was utterly incapable of deciding which task was the most urgent, so she swept her desk clean and did what she always did when life blindsided her one time too many.

She took a sheet of personal stationery and began—actually, began again—a letter she had spent most of her life trying to write.

More than twenty-five years had passed since she began framing the words in her mind. Larabeth was at ease speaking on television, to political figures, to the rich, to the influential. She had written dozens of articles for academic and popular presses. But she was left inarticulate by the thought of introducing herself to the daughter she had never seen.

❖ ◆ ❖ ◆ ❖

Four sheets of stationery lay crumpled in Larabeth's wastebasket. There was still no graceful way to say, *You don't know me, but I'm your mother*. She had thought it would be easier, that someday she would have the maturity and perspective to finally introduce herself to the girl. No, she corrected herself, to introduce herself to Cynthia. She had a name, even if it wasn't the one Larabeth would have chosen for her.

She put her pen away and retrieved a pair of jeans from her desk drawer. There was no more sure cure for a hard day than a long drive in a classic Mustang with the top down.

She slung her jacket over one shoulder and bolted for the elevator, closing her mind to the piles of work on her desk. Norma was gone for the day and the hall was empty except for a slight, fiftyish maintenance man limping behind a garbage bin. Larabeth, well-bred Southerner that she was, smiled and nodded as she passed him. He acknowledged her smile without quite catching her eye and continued his deliberate progress down the hall.

The man paused as Larabeth disappeared behind the elevator doors. He reached into his bin and gently drew out a length of discarded strapping tape. It wasn't a showy weapon but, wrapped properly and quickly around a neck, it would suffice. He had made do with less.

Killing Larabeth on the spot would have been pleasurable, and it would have been easy. But it wasn't part of the plan, at least not now. Babykiller had patience and he had brains, and those two things alone had been enough to earn him a fortune and to keep him alive. He let the tape drop into the bin.

He reached in his pocket and withdrew a pair of sheer rubber gloves and a key. He let himself into the door stenciled with the words: BioHeal—Fifteen Years of Service to Industry, Government, and the Earth. It had been a long time since he did his own legwork but, for Larabeth—well, nothing was too good for Larabeth.

He perused the documents on Norma's desk, then moved into Larabeth's office. He ignored her computer. There was nothing there he couldn't access from the comfort of his own home. No, he was checking for hard-copy information, and Larabeth's wastebasket held the jackpot. He skimmed four crumpled pieces of stationery as he dumped the remaining trash into his bin.

A daughter. Not only did he know Larabeth had a daughter, now he had her name and address. He threw the letters into his rolling bin and began rifling through Larabeth's files. As soon as he got to his car, he would call Gerald and have him tail the daughter, peer into her shadowy closets, chase her into a trap she couldn't even see. Then he would see whether Larabeth was made of sand or stone.

This was too easy, but that would change. Larabeth was too smart to leave herself open to his feeblest tricks. She would learn, but not soon enough. He would win.

Chapter 2

The Mississippi River crawled beneath Larabeth's baby-girl pink '67 Mustang convertible. Downtown New Orleans was behind her, out of sight and out of mind, as long as she ignored the image of the Superdome in her rear-view mirror.

It was a relief to cross the river. The daily act of putting a broad, deep, muddy force of nature between herself and the corporate world felt good. Descending from the great span and passing the toll booths, she made an executive decision to skip the gym, for once. A swift drive through the rural area around Belle Chasse would do far more to calm her nerves.

As she pulled into her garage, she found that the Mustang cure had worked again. Maintenance costs on two thirty-year-old cars could be steep, but they were surely cheaper than a therapist, and far less nosy. Summer in New Orleans was an interminable curse, but at least she could put the top down and drive away her troubles most of the year, as long as she stayed alert for the other curse of the subtropics, afternoon thundershowers.

There would be just time for supper before she caught herself on the evening news. She hoped her orange suit photographed well and that the cameras didn't reveal any lipstick on her teeth.

She kicked her shoes off in the laundry room and rummaged in the dryer for a clean tee-shirt. Going straight to the kitchen and piling ham on a slice of whole wheat, she threw caution to the wind and laid the mayonnaise on thick. Thinking that a bowl of soup would taste good with the cold sandwich, she listened to the familiar pop-whir of the electric can-opener, dumped the tomato soup in a pot, then held the can under the faucet without looking.

The water spurted out with a strange gurgle. Not another plumbing problem, Larabeth prayed. She glanced at the sink, then looked again. Her water was green. Not pale green and not the natural green of a swimming pool gone bad. It was the sick green Hollywood uses in its fake toxic waste.

The unnatural fluid overtopped the soup can and flowed onto her hand. She let the can clatter into the sink, jerking her hand away and shutting the faucet off.

The fluid didn't burn her hand, at least not yet. There was no smell and no sticky or slimy feel to it. Nevertheless, Larabeth wanted her hand clean. Immediately.

She wiped it on a paper towel, picked up a bar of soap, then reflexively turned on the faucet and stuck her hands under the flow. It was still green.

"You idiot," she muttered as she jerked them away and reached for more paper towels. "Stupid, stupid, stupid. When the nuclear holocaust comes, you'll be the last woman on earth to stop reaching for a light switch at sundown."

Larabeth tossed the paper towels in the garbage. She was an environmental scientist. While her specialty was soil bioremediation, she could hold her own when it came to drinking water treatment. She could think of no plausible way for the local treatment plant to create water in that shade of green, but she guessed stranger things were possible. She could also think of no plausible explanation for her kitchen sink to go haywire unless water in the other areas of her house was also affected.

She was, however, scientist enough to check her other sinks. Maybe the water ran a different color in each bathroom. Maybe she was in Oz and her kitchen was the Emerald City. Maybe the water in the master bath was blue and Glenda the Good Witch was waiting there with a kiss and a pair of silver slippers. Maybe her water was like the tonic in Mary Poppins's carpetbag, turning whatever color or flavor you chose—although she frankly would never have chosen slime green. Or maybe she just needed to get a grip.

She left her kitchen sink to its steady green drip-drip and checked all three bathroom sinks. She checked the showers and tubs, even the whirlpool tub in the master bath. She flushed the toilets, ran water into the washing machine, checked the dishwasher and the icemaker. Nothing. Everything ran fresh and clear but the kitchen sink.

She studied the offending faucet for a while. Drip. Still green. Drip. Still green. It hadn't been dripping that morning. She had repaired many a leaky faucet in her day. She didn't see how a worn-out washer could cause this problem, but scientists did like to take things apart and see how they worked.

She reached into the drawer where she kept her household tools. It occurred to her that when she got the faucet dismantled, her hands would be covered with the green water. She didn't have any kitchen gloves, so she slipped a couple of large plastic bags over her hands and went to work.

Turning the shutoff valve under the sink and taking a wrench to the faucet, she lifted the stem assembly out and turned it over. The screw holding in the washer slipped out in her hands and the washer, covered in green goo, fell into the sink. There was a wet plop, but no metal-on-porcelain clink.

Larabeth picked up the semi-solid mass of green, cradling it in her palm. It had been a temporary washer, crafted out of a powdered dye and designed to dissolve slowly into running water. If she had allowed the water to run much longer, it would have dissolved away completely, leaving her with a sink dribbling clear water.

The solution to the green-water mystery was so interesting, it took Larabeth a full minute to realize the implications. Someone had tampered with her drinking water. She was more violated by the thought than she would have expected.

She looked around the kitchen to see if anything else was askew and she saw it—a tampering so subtle only the person who last used the kitchen would recognize it.

She had left the kitchen clean. She always left the kitchen clean. There had been nothing in the sink. She knew the counters had been bare, because she had wiped every surface clean. Yet now there was a cleaver in the sink, a butcher knife beside the cooktop, and a paring knife posed casually on the chopping board as if expecting the chef to return at any time.

She checked her knife block. It was empty. Every sharp implement she owned had been painstakingly arrayed around her kitchen. A glint on the windowsill caught her eye. She moved closer and found the kitchen scissors amongst her herb garden, as if poised to clip a few sprigs of chives.

This was bizarre. She would need to call the police. They would want to investigate the breaking-and-entering, and they would need to analyze the dye residue. She wasn't sure what they would think about the knives. Maybe they could get some fingerprints. Or maybe they'd just think she was a sloppy housekeeper with a bad memory. Nevertheless, the police must be called.

Larabeth was not one to turn over her well-being to anyone, no matter how professional or well-intentioned. She got a small plastic bag and, with a clean spoon, carefully raked into it a gob of green goo from the dye tablet she had removed from her faucet. Now she could hand the police an essentially intact piece of evidence while retaining a sample to analyze at BioHeal's in-house lab. There was no sense in risking a faulty analysis or a lost sample. Her chemists were accurate and reliable, and they would do the work in a fraction of the time.

She had tucked the sample in the refrigerator when the telephone rang.

“Did you watch yourself on TV, Doc?” It was him, the crank caller. She was not particularly surprised to find he knew her unlisted home number.

“I've been busy," she said coolly. "I may catch it on the late news.”

“I hear you have a nice house, Doc. Lots of windows. Lots of land. A long way to your nearest neighbor. I understand you live there alone.” Larabeth reflexively reached up and closed the blinds over her kitchen window. She immediately felt foolish.

“If you're threatening me, it won't work,” she said. “I may have been careless in the past, but no more. If you know so much about me, you know I can afford a security system, a gun, even a personal security guard, if that's what it takes. What is it that you want?"

"Calm down, Doc. I'm not threatening you. At the moment, I just want to talk to you. You do such interesting work. Biological treatment of contaminated soils. That, my dear, is a very lucrative mouthful, isn't it? Everybody loves what you do, Doc. For the polluters caught with their pants down, your cleanup strategy (patented, of course) is quicker and cheaper than any other game in town. The bunny-hugging environmentalists love you because your strategy doesn't use any inconvenient toxic chemicals, it doesn't pollute the air, and it doesn't require the construction of a landfill in anybody's back yard."

"Like I said this morning, you're not saying anything that hasn't been in the papers a dozen times," she said, doggedly putting her knives away. Fancy wood-handled butcher knives in the block. Paring knife in its own self-sharpening sheath. Non-fancy ugly knives in the drawer. If she kept her hands busy, she wouldn't have to think.

"Larabeth, you are a feisty thing," the cool voice continued. "I like that. But I digress. I'm also interested in your less well-known work. You were once quite well-versed on the Agent Orange debacle—where it was used, who was exposed, how it affects the body."

"That was long ago, in graduate school." The last knife slipped safely into its slot. "Congratulations. You've uncovered an obscure part of my past, but it's hardly a state secret. Am I supposed to be impressed? You won't even give me your name. We're hardly on an equal footing here."

"I am completely uninterested in putting our—shall we call it a relationship?—our relationship on an equal footing." The retort was quick and firm. There was no apparent change in the man's level, well-modulated tone, but Larabeth was chilled. She could tell he wanted her to be. "I will be magnanimous, however, and give you a name. Not my given name—I last used my given name in 1982—but one you will understand. You may call me Babykiller."

Larabeth winced. She'd never been so unlucky as to be called a babykiller, but she knew many Vietnam vets who had. She hadn't heard that epithet in years. "So you were in Vietnam. So was I and so were a few hundred thousand other lost souls. What do you expect me to do with that information?"

"You can do whatever you like with it. You're quite adept at using information. Your graduate work on Agent Orange, for example. You amassed an impressive database, with precious little cooperation from our caring government. You knew more about our herbicide spraying program than the VA itself. They knew a good thing when they saw it. They're using your data for their own purposes these days."

"I'm not surprised. Babykiller, tell me something. We've had quite a long conversation. Aren't you afraid it's being traced?"

"You should know by now that I don't answer direct questions. Use your beautiful head. There are a limited number of possibilities. Maybe I know for sure you don't have the equipment. Maybe I'm taking a calculated risk that you don't have the equipment. Maybe I don't care if you find me. Or maybe there's no way to trace me, even if you do have the equipment. I'll give you a few hints. I am older and wiser than you. I do care if you find me, and I don't take calculated risks. And with those jewels of wisdom, Doc, I really must go, but I'll leave you with a parting thought."

He paused for effect. She listened for sounds of breathing and heard none.

"If I were you," he continued, "I would read the morning paper religiously. You may find me there—or you may see where I've been. Stay close to the phone, Doc."

The receiver was hardly back in the cradle when the phone rang again. She snatched it up without thinking. Then, afraid Babykiller was on the line again, she heard herself answer in an oddly timid voice.

"Larabeth? You sound different. I guess it's been a long time."

Larabeth made an effort to sound like herself. "J.D., you're right, it has been a long time. And there are some things we need to discuss. For instance, I owe you an apology. But right now, I need to get down to business. I've had three frightening phone calls today and someone has broken into my house."

"I'm calling from my car. I can be right over. What did they take?"

"Nothing, so far as I can tell, but they left some things. I've been given a warning."

J.D.'s tone grew firm. "There's no such thing as just a warning. Have you been in every room in your house since you got home? Are there any closets or shower stalls where someone could be hiding?"

"I've been in most of the house, but not every room. Shower stalls—no, nobody could be in there. I've looked. Closets, maybe, but most of them are too full for someone to hide in."

"I assume you still live in the same house."

"Yes," she said quietly.

"Where are you now?"

"In the kitchen." She didn't add, *Crouched on the linoleum*.

"I'll call the police. Until I get there or they do, get down where no one can see you through the windows.

Don't answer the phone unless you screen it through your answering machine. Do you have Caller ID?"

"I'm not that paranoid. At least I wasn't before now."

"And Larabeth—if anyone breaks in, they could be armed. Reach up and pull a kitchen knife out of a drawer, but only if you think you could use it if you had to. If you don't, leave it where it is. Too many people have been killed with weapons they were afraid to use. I'm going to hang up now and call the police."

The line went silent.

Larabeth didn't budge from the floor. She reached up beside the cooktop and found the butcher knife she wanted. It was old and it had been sharpened many times. The worn handle was unsightly next to the cleaned and oiled chef's knives that she owned but didn't use. Most of all, it was huge. She crouched, waiting, and felt the edge of the blade. J.D. was concerned that she didn't have the guts to use it. J.D. didn't know the half of it.

There was little in the way of cover or camouflage on the floor of her kitchen. It was true, she was well-hidden from anyone trying to shoot through her window, but if someone got into the house or if someone already was in the house, she wouldn't go undiscovered for long.

Larabeth loved her house. She had supervised every step of the remodeling, exulting every time an interior wall came down or a new window went in. She had furnished it in "the colors God gave us", to use an interior designer's pretentious phrase: soft beiges, foamy blues, ocean greens. The resulting home was delightfully soothing—all light and glass and open spaces—but it was not designed for hiding from prowlers.

Nothing separated her from the great open core of the house but a low cooking island. Larabeth adjusted her grip on the knife's handle and wondered whether her home would ever look calm, welcoming, or safe again.

Wounded Earth *is available in all ebook formats and in print.*

A WORD OF FAREWELL

Thank you for helping me rummage through my jewel box, enjoying the bright colors and sparkling facets of the gems that live there. I have so enjoyed reminding myself how much I love stories. I love the things they say, and I love the things they don't say. And I enjoy the company of others who appreciate what stories do for us.

Happy reading to you all...

What People are Saying About Mary Anna Evans' Fiction

For short story "Land of the Flowers", published in *A Merry Band of Murderers*:

"...Three [stories] are particularly noteworthy: Mary Anna Evans' *Land of the Flowers*, Jeffrey Deaver's *The Fan*, and Val McDermid's *Long Black Veil.... A Merry Band of Murderers* is an admirable anthology of short stories by a skilled company of mystery authors."

—Mysterious Reviews

For environmental thriller *Wounded Earth*:

"Its nail-biting intensity will keep you up late in your eagerness to find out how it ends."

—Big Al's Books and Pals

For Florida Book Awards Bronze Medalist *Effigies*:

"We mystery lovers who've enjoyed Artifacts and thought Relics was even better may not believe this, but Ms. Evans has done it again, and Effigies is the best one yet. Again, she makes a lesson in our past a fascinating read."

—Tony Hillerman, recipient of the Mystery Writers of America's Grand Master Award, and the Navajo Tribe's Special Friend Award, among many other honors.

For *Offerings*, winner of Red Adept's 2010 Indie Award for best collection:

"Very much recommended, very much impressed..."

—Red Adept Book Reviews

For Benjamin Franklin Award-winner *Artifacts*:

"It's always fun to discover a new Florida voice, especially one who can bring to life the rich texture—the sand, the sea, the moss-draped live oaks, the seedy fishing shacks, the salted boat culture—of the state's coast...the menace and the history are resolved in a hurricane of a finale."

—Tampa Tribune

For IMBA Bestseller *Relics*:

"A fascinating look at contemporary archaeology but also a twisted story of greed and its effects."

—Dallas Morning News

About the Author

MARY ANNA EVANS is the author of the award-winning Faye Longchamp archaeological mysteries: *Artifacts, Relics, Effigies, Findings, Floodgates, Strangers*, and *Plunder*. She's a chemical engineer by training and license, with a degree in engineering physics thrown in for spice, but she loves reading about history and writing about an archaeologist. Truth be told, she's a little jealous of Faye and her archaeological adventures.

She enjoys reading, writing, gardening, spending time with her family, cooking, and playing her 7-and-a-half-foot-long monster of a grand piano. Her cat helps her write, so she should probably put his name on her books. Learn more about Mary Anna and her work here:

Website:
http://www.maryannaevans.com

Facebook:
http://www.facebook.com/pages/Mary-Anna-Evans-auhor-of-the-Faye-Longchamp-archaeological-mysteries/8113134580

CPSIA information can be obtained
at www.ICGtesting.com
Printed in the USA
LVHW01s0100100817
544461LV00009B/69/P